Regression

Trish Harland

DEDICATION

For Heather and Jean both lifelong friends and who, like all true friends, accept me for who I am warts and all.

ACKNOWLEDGMENTS

First and foremost I would like to thank Elaine Collier who has been my critic, my editor and last but not least my inspiration for writing this my second novel in the Jake Summers series.

I would also like to thank Kitty Phillips for her insight into all things spiritual.

Other Books by Trish Harland

Jake Summers Series
Dead Ringers

Short Stories
Misconceptions

DISCLAIMER

A Jake Summers Novel

What a man has made himself he will be; his state is the result of his past life, and his heaven or hell is in himself.
~ *Catherine Crowe*

There were a billion lights out there on the horizon and I knew that all of them put together weren't enough to light the darkness in the hearts of some men.
~ *Michael Connelly, The Scarecrow*

PROLOGUE

The soft melodic voice that brought me here was insistent, urging me to open the old rough- hewn door that stood in front of me. The year 1884 AD was carved into a plaque nailed to the door. Probably what lay behind it held the secret of my past and inevitably my future? Excited and somewhat apprehensive I pushed it open and walked inside. Immediately I knew that I was back, back home, the home in which I truly belonged.

"Do you know your name and where you are?", the voice prompted.

"My name is Jeb Carter, I'm 28-years-old and I'm standing in the hallway of my farm cottage."

"And do you know where the cottage is Jeb?"

"Stanton, a village in the North Riding of Yorkshire."

Kate was amazed and delighted; her client even had an authentic Yorkshire accent.

"And the year Jeb, do you know the year?"

"It's July, 1884."

"And how are you dressed?"

I glanced down and began to describe my rustic clothing.

"I'm wearing long black pants with button fly, held up by braces which are mostly hidden by an ill-fitting waistcoat made from the same coarse material as the trousers. An off-white collarless shirt is

1

tucked into my trousers and I have mud covered brown boots on my feet."

"And your surroundings Jeb, can you describe them? " Her voice, still soft, sounded excited and somehow more insistent, as if she wanted to know everything and was enjoying the experience with me.

"To my left a door opens into the front parlour; the room is kept in pristine condition although it's only ever used on high days and holidays. I don't need to open the door to describe the room and its contents, it's firmly ingrained in my memory. It's always cool because the fire's unlit for most of the year. I remember my wife Jane's parents furnishing it for us when we moved in, insisting that their daughter should have at least one decent room in the hovel she now called home. They don't approve of me, never have. After all I'm just a farm worker with no money and no prospects and she was the daughter of Tristan Metcalfe, grocer and vice chairman of the school board and his wife Hannah daughter of Richard Monkman of Glebe farm.

Jane (or Ginny as I call her) defied her parents and married me. Her grandfather Richard, who farms 400-acres of arable land in Stanton, took me on as an agricultural labourer and provided us with this cottage on the edge of his estate.

At the end of the narrow hallway in which I'm standing is a staircase that leads to two first floor bedrooms. One small sparsely furnished single and ours, which has a double size iron bedstead with feather mattress, a washstand and a large cupboard containing shelves. On the ground floor, opposite the staircase, is the scullery. Here Ginny would cook our meals over the coal fired range, wash our clothes and sit at the small wooden table and sew. In fact she would spend most of her day in here just being a good wife. Through the kitchen door there's a well which provides our water and 10-yards beyond an outside privy."

Kate, overwhelmed by the detailed descriptions given without her constant prompting, was nonetheless puzzled by the past tense references to his wife.

"Is Ginny there now Jeb?"

At the mention of his wife he became agitated and began to laugh uncontrollably.

Suddenly he stopped, sat upright and yelled "Whore".

Shocked by his vehement outburst, Kate decided now was a good time to bring her client back to the present.

"So Jeb relax now," she said calmly, "it's time to leave your cottage, to retrace your steps closing the door firmly behind you."

'Dream on lady,' I thought, 'I've been awakened, me, Jeb Carter, and I'm not about to abandon my past so readily.' Gleefully I left the door wide open as her voice coaxed me back to the twenty-first century.

1

David Mitchell seemed very different from the mild mannered guy with the downcast eyes who'd walked into her life just an hour ago. Kate found it unnerving as he stared at her with pale blue unblinking eyes as they discussed his past life regression experience. Anxious to see the back of him, Kate stood.

"So Mr Mitchell, if you have no further questions just leave your address with me and I'll send you the recording and notes I made during your session."

"Thank you Kate, very enjoyable and enlightening, money well spent."

Kate almost grimaced at the overfamiliar use of her Christian name but, always the professional, instead she offered him her hand.

He smiled knowingly as he took her outstretched hand and held it just a little too long for her liking.

"Almost forgot," he said, handing her a card with his name and address. "I look forward to receiving the package." And with that parting quip he turned and left.

Kate let out a long sigh as the door closed behind him. She heard his steps on the stairs, moved to the window and, thankfully, saw him leave the building and disappear down the road.

Kate had qualified as a Past Life Regression Hypnotherapist just six months ago and David Mitchell was the first client that was a stranger to her. Until now they'd all been known to her, friends,

friends of friends, family and acquaintances.

The session with Mitchell, aka Jeb Carter, went well until she'd mentioned his wife and then it was if a light bulb had been switched on in his brain and changed his personality; and that change had followed him back to the present. She'd found the change intimidating.

"Only I could net a weirdo first time out," she muttered cynically.

The thing she'd learned most about today's experience was that you don't offer appointments to strangers when your business partner is not keeping shop downstairs.

Kate met Linda Benson three years ago in 2011. She'd enrolled in a meditation class hoping that it would help her get over her cheating ex, Rhys Davis. The bastard just couldn't keep it in his trousers, she'd forgiven him once but twice he was having a laugh. Linda was her meditation teacher and they clicked immediately, became firm friends and when a year later Kate decided she needed a career change they decided to go into business together and Shades of Indigo was born. They rented a period property for a peppercorn rent of £100 per month from Linda's wealthy father-in-law, Walt Benson. Located at 3 Brookland Avenue in Newbury, the property was arranged over three floors. The avenue was well known for its specialist retail shops and professional services. A single fronted shop on the ground floor was their retail outlet for Linda's love of all things crystal, selling everything from handmade jewellery to polished tumble stones. The second floor had three rooms which they used for holistic therapies, past life regression and meditation teaching. Kate lived on the third floor in a one-bedroomed apartment which she had modernised before moving in. Linda lived with her husband Mike and two daughters just a five minute walk away. The two women, intent on making their business successful, learned a whole range of holistic therapies and spiritual awareness techniques to offer to their clients. The first year was tough but things were really beginning to take off now and they were beginning to reap the rewards of their hard work.

Kate went downstairs unlocked the adjoining door into the shop and prepared for what she hoped would be a successful afternoon in retail sales.

***

Feeling empowered I walked away with a swagger in my step. I could feel Kate Davis watching as I left and I resisted the temptation to turn, smile and wave to her. Already spooked by the change in my personality, it wasn't a good idea to give her even more reason to remember me. However, the thought made me smile. The false address meant I'd never receive the session recording but hey, I didn't need it, I had what I came for. Who the hell was David Mitchell anyway, just a name on a gravestone in Newtown Park Cemetery.

2

JEB CARTER

I stood at the kitchen door looking over the field of ripening corn watching it dance playfully in the freshening breeze. Despite the breeze it was a warm, summer evening and I remembered it was on an evening much like this that I brought my Ginny home. She was my Ginny then, fresh faced, beautiful and truly happy to be my bride. Left to our own devices I'm sure we would be happy to this day but her interfering parents just wouldn't let us be. It was the day the piano arrived in our parlour, bought and paid for by the high and mighty Tristan Metcalfe. I came home from work, no dinner on the table and Ginny in the parlour playing the cursed instrument. She heard me come in and excitedly turned to greet me.

"Look what daddy bought for us, isn't it marvellous?"

"My dinner on the table would be marvellous and it was bought for you not us, I don't play the bloody piano."

Realising I was angry, she immediately got up, walked towards me and kissed my cheek.

"Sorry about dinner darling, I just got carried away with the joy of playing again."

I pushed her away and glared.

"I suppose you'd rather be living the life of a lady again, not sharing this hovel with me."

She looked hurt.

"Don't be stupid Jeb Carter, I love you. There will always be aspects of my old life that I miss but I chose to be with you. Surely that doesn't mean I have to give up all the other things I love."

That's when I hit her; a backhanded blow to the side of her face knocked her to the ground.

"Don't ever call me stupid again."

She looked up at me in disbelief, her eyes brimming with tears.

"I'll be back in one hour, just make sure my dinner's on the table by then."

I left the house and walked the half mile to the Taverner's Arms where I spent the next hour supping ale I could ill afford.

Of course I apologised for my behaviour but in reality the incident empowered me. For the first time I felt like the master in my own home and by God I'd make sure she knew it too. Just like my father before me I'd rule my roost with a rod of iron.

I never made the mistake of marking her face again, just too difficult to explain away. All my blows were aimed at the body, so any bruising was hidden from prying eyes. Instead of feeling guilty about the beatings I felt horny and so ultimately the physical abuse led to sexual abuse. I raped my wife and enjoyed it.

I knew she was too ashamed to tell her parents, now cowed and submissive I'd finally knocked that privileged lifestyle out of her. I never heard her play again.

The memory evoked a powerful response and my sexual arousal was immediate and obvious but, of course, she was no longer there to satisfy my basic needs. She and her lover were rotting together beneath that dancing corn.

They say the husband is always the last to know and in this case they were right. The gossipmongers in the village were delighting in the burgeoning friendship between my wife and Frederick Simmons, the local schoolmaster. I had no idea that the bitch was cheating on me until incessant rain drove me home early that fateful day. I found them cosying up together in our parlour. I left the room without a word, grabbed my axe from outside came back and decapitated Frederick bloody Simmons with a single blow. A fountain of blood covered them both. The shock and desperation in her eyes did nothing to dispel my anger as I swung the axe a second time and buried it in her skull. I stood over the bodies and smiled.

"No one messes with Jeb Carter."

I buried them together in the field behind the house, her first then him on top just as I'd found them. It took me hours of scrubbing to clean all the blood from the quarry tiles in the parlour. Two weeks later I planted the corn that grew there now. The next evening I went to the pub and told everyone who would listen that my cheating wife had run off with the bloody schoolmaster. No one disbelieved me, the gossipmongers had done a good job. Everyone felt sorry for poor old Jeb Carter, cuckolded by an uppity wife. If only they knew..

3

Zoe Dryden watched her sleeping son and smiled. Seven-year-old Zak was a smaller, paler version of the man who spawned him. She'd met Carlson Cambridge at University. Not a fellow student but an employee at the Student Union Bar. Hailing from St Vincent in the Caribbean, he had all the laid back charm and charisma that men from the West Indies can often exhibit. He was tall, handsome, with unusual green eyes that immediately captured her interest. A pencil moustache adorned his upper lip and she was reminded of a darker, younger, Terence Howard who was one of her favourite actors. Like most good barmen, he had the chat that went with the looks. From the moment they met, those amazing eyes singled her out from the crowd of good looking girls surrounding the bar. Unable to resist his magnetic appeal she soon found herself embroiled in a passionate love affair. A considerate, experienced lover, Carlson taught Zoe the true meaning of passion. They spent seven idyllic months together. Idyllic until she discovered she was pregnant. Within a week he had scuttled back to the Caribbean leaving her heartbroken and alone. His friend Rich, another barman, told her that he had a wife and kid back in St. Vincent.

"Surely you knew," Rich said.

"If I'd known I'd have steered clear of any sort of involvement. Why didn't you tell me?"

"Not my business," Rich shrugged, "and anyway, most students have the morals of alley cats."

"Thanks! But I'm not most students."

"Sorry love, but boys will be boys, live with it," he shrugged again and moved away to serve another half pissed customer.

"Charming," she shouted after him but to no avail. How dare he imply she had the morals of an alley cat? What about Carlson's morals? She'd assumed, wrongly it seemed, that he was free and single.

She did the only thing she could; she jacked in her course and went home to mum and dad. Far from being supportive they insisted she get a termination. Having an illegitimate child was bad enough but a mixed race illegitimate child was tantamount to insanity. What would the neighbours think?

What the hell did she care what the neighbours thought, there was no way she would abort her baby.

Her father gave her an ultimatum "Get rid or get out."

Even her mother looked shocked, but Zoe knew there wasn't a hope in hell that she'd go against his decision, she never had before and wasn't about to change the habit of a lifetime now. Always a homemaker, she just kept the peace and did her husband's bidding.

Determined to keep her unborn child, she packed her bags and arrived on her married sister Diana's doorstep. She hoped Diana would take pity on her, at least until the baby was born and she could get back on her feet and support them both. Diana made all the right noises but her husband Rob wasn't happy and she could hear them arguing about her in the kitchen.

"She's my sister, she's in trouble and she's staying here until she's sorted."

"So we're saddled with her and her kid until she decides she's sorted?"

"She can help with the boys, think of the money we'll save on child care."

Money always motivated Rob and suddenly it wasn't such a bad idea.

"Well there is that I suppose, okay she can stay until the kid's born. What I don't want is months of being woken at night by a screaming baby that's not even ours, we've only just put that scenario to bed ourselves."

Diana came out of the kitchen smiling and gave Zoe the thumbs up.

Zoe still remembered the relief that flowed through her and the gratitude she felt. They lived together in relative harmony until Zak was born. Even Rob got used to her being there and, of course, the extra money in his pocket was always a good incentive. Nothing was said about her moving out but Zoe was determined to get work and make a home for her and Zak. He started sleeping through the night at just five-months-old so she took a job at a local bar and club as a waitress. The hours were good, 7:30pm to 1am so she could look after Diana's boys during the day and work evenings while Zak slept.

She soon realised that the club was really a classy bordello where rich men came to dine with friends and buy an evening of pleasure with the good looking hostesses.

Realising that she couldn't rely on her sister's hospitality indefinitely, she got drawn into the seedy well paid world of sex for money. Clients found her dark hair, brown eyes and curvaceous figure an alluring contrast to the angular honed bodies of the blonde Eastern Europeans that made up 75% of the club's working girls. Cora Allen, the 55-year-old owner was a former working girl herself, she'd been left money in a wealthy client's will allowing her to move from Manchester and buy the Blue Lagoon Club here in Newbury.

On the ground floor a cordon bleu restaurant and bar provided fine food and drink. A separate lounge bar allowed customers to come in for a quiet drink in luxurious surroundings. Nightly entertainment was provided by Scarlet Danvers, a 35-year-old, no-nonsense, fiery redhead who played piano and sang classic ballads in a deep soulful voice, reminiscent of Aretha Franklin. Scarlet made it abundantly clear to any amorous punters that she was completely off limits, besides her husband Nick was the bar manager and wouldn't tolerate any nonsense from the customers.

The first floor had ten en-suite bedrooms which the girls rented for £200 a day. Any money they made was theirs so she couldn't be closed down for running a knocking shop, albeit a high class one. Her fairness with the girls had earned her total respect and loyalty. Cora had a fabulous four roomed apartment on the top floor and, without doubt, the whole place spelled CLASS in capital letters. Within a year Zoe (or Candice as she was known at the club) was making in excess of £1000 a week and was able to put down a deposit on a 3-bedroomed house in a decent neighbourhood; a place where Zak could go to a good school, make nice friends and somewhere completely divorced from her working environment and, most importantly, where nobody knew how she earned a living.

Zak grunted in his sleep, interrupting her thoughts. She noticed the open book on the floor. It must have slipped from his grasp as he drifted off to sleep. Bending down she picked it up and was amazed to find that her seven-year-old was actually reading Treasure Island. 'Clever as well as handsome' she thought.

The doorbell rang downstairs..

4

JEB CARTER

I watched Olivia King unhook the tin bath from the back of the barn door and carry it towards the timber frame house that stood on the edge of Anderley woods. I stepped out of the shadows at the side of the barn and moved to the scullery window where I watched as she pulled the table to one side and lit the oil lamp that stood on it. She pulled the bath into the space in front of the fire and began to fill it with pans of water heating on the black leaded grate. Friday night was bath night; it was also the night that husband Henry helped out at the Taverner's Arms. He wouldn't be home until after 11pm. I knew, I'd been here many times before. As the sky darkened outside, the scullery took on a soft warm glow. I watched as she stripped off her clothes, slowly, tantalisingly, as if she knew I was there watching. She lifted her leg, tested the water with her outstretched foot, satisfied she stepped in and sank down into it. Aroused and feeling the swelling in my groin pushing for release, I knew it was time to claim my prize. She closed her eyes, relaxing into the comforting warmth that enveloped her. Soundlessly I opened the door and crept up behind her.

Kneeling down I whispered "does Henry know you're entertaining tonight?"

Startled her eyes flew open and she desperately tried to cover her naked breasts with her hands.

I laughed.

"Too late darling, I've seen it all and by God Livie, I like what I see."

She turned, I could see the terror in her eyes as she saw my erection.

"Jeb Carter, what the hell do you think you're doing? Why are you here?"

The panic in her voice aroused me more and running a hand over the bulge in my pants I said, "Surely it's obvious, I'm here to fuck you senseless."

She stood up defiantly, grabbed a towel from the line above her head and wrapped it around her.

I stood too and roughly pulling the towel away, captured her in my arms and lifted her dripping body from the bath.

Putting her down on the home made rag rug, I felt her struggling against me and then she started to scream. I let go with my right hand put my finger to my lips.

"Sssshh Livie, no one can hear you."

Deciding to appeal to my better nature she looked me in the eye.

"Why are you being like this Jeb? The four of us were good friends when Ginny was here."

"No Livie, you and Ginny were friends, I was just the husband who tagged along. Now she's gone, you're here, and it's been a long time since I've had a woman. Guess it's your lucky day, I've chosen you."

"You won't get away with it, Henry will kill you."

"Livie, Livie, Henry will never know."

Realisation registered and she screamed.

"You're mad."

"Big mistake Livie," I hissed through clenched teeth as I knocked her to the floor.

"No-one calls me mad."

Stunned by the blow she lay on her back on the rug, mine for the taking. Quickly, shucking off my pants and kneeling over her, I forced her legs apart and slid into her tight unyielding body. As I began to pump she came to and started to scream and struggle. Holding her arms above her head with one hand I put the over her mouth. I was determined to finish what I'd started and give my body the release it craved. I bent close to her ear and whispered.

"Be a good girl Livie, just relax and enjoy it."

As I climaxed I felt her body go limp beneath me. Finally spent I sighed, rolled off her, looked down and realised she wasn't breathing.

"Dead already? How inconsiderate Livie, I was hoping to use you again before I killed you."

Feeling no remorse I dressed and began the process of cleaning up. Just like Ginny, Olivia King was about to disappear without trace. Knowing I had to be thorough, I dragged the bath outside, emptied it behind the barn and carried it back inside to dry by the fire. Then I went upstairs, gathered up her clothes, dresses hanging from hooks behind the bedroom door, undergarments and nightdresses from the chest of drawers and two pairs of shoes from under the bed, and shoved them into a canvas bag that I'd seen Henry use when we were out shooting rabbits.

I buried her body and clothes deep in Anderley Wood where I was sure it wouldn't be discovered.

The bath was back in the barn, the table back in front of the fire, the oil lamp turned off and I was on my way back home with a spring in my step and her necklace in my pocket. We would all commiserate with Henry when he told us that Livie had left him..

5

Jake Summers felt as if his lungs were about to collapse. The pressure on his chest was unbearable, something heavy was pinning him to the floor. His very existence depended on getting out from under it but he couldn't move. The phone rang. Jake woke to the reality that Hobbs, his large marmalade cat, was laying at full stretch on top of the bed and him.

"Dammit Hobbs, I thought I was dying," he said, as he rolled over to answer the persistent ringing. The cat, annoyed at being disturbed, just muttered and moved to the end of the bed.

Jake glanced over at Jaime who was still asleep and wondered at her ability to sleep through almost anything.

He picked up the phone.

"Summers," he said abruptly.

"Jake its Mo." DI Mo Connolly was his friend, his almost relative and his second in command at Newbury Police Headquarters.

"Do you know what the time is?" he asked, picking his watch up from the bedside table. "This had better be good."

"My old friend Cora Allen's been on the blower, apparently one of her girls hasn't shown at the club for the last three nights and she's worried. She hadn't even had a phone call from her and that's unusual because this girl's always so reliable. She's a single mum, living in a nice area on the south side of town, and needs the money. Probably nothing, but you know what a fusspot Cora can be so I agreed to check it out. We're on our way to Birchfield Avenue now, I've got Dave with me. So this is just a courtesy call to let you know we're not skiving. Sorry if I interrupted anything."

"Nothing at all Connolly," Jake laughed, "and if you're skiving it's a great story just to get an extra hour in bed."

"Well you have to be inventive with such a sharp DCI in charge. Go back to bed, I'll see you later."

"No chance, I'm awake now," he said, putting down the phone and jumping out of bed, disturbing Jaime as he did.

"Sorry darling, police work beckons."

"Better put some clothes on before you leave," she said, looking up at his naked body and positively leering. "That's definitely for my eyes only."

"Bond, James Bond," he said, dropping to his knees and pretending to point a gun in her direction.

She laughed out loud.

"You look ridiculous."

"I know, but it made you laugh."

He scrambled to his feet walked over to the bed, bent down and kissed her forehead.

"I'd ask you to join me in the shower but then such intimate contact with such a foxy lady will make me horribly late."

"Much too early anyway," she said, turning her back on him and closing her eyes.

She heard his car drive away about ten minutes later and rolling onto her back stretched languidly, disturbing Hobbs in the process.

The cat grumbled and Jaime laughed.

"Jake thinks we should keep you out of the bedroom," she said, reaching out to stroke the disgruntled moggie. "But that would be tantamount to eviction now wouldn't it?" Big green eyes looked up at her and she could feel him purring beneath her hand. The large marmalade cat had adopted Jake when he lived in Donnington. Despite protests otherwise, Jake loved this bossy old tom cat and that wasn't difficult, she'd quickly grown to love him too.

She'd become Mrs Jake Summers six months ago and they'd moved into their beautiful home two weeks later. It was a new build located on the edge of Leckhampstead, a village in West Berkshire about 8-miles northwest of Newbury. Convenient for Jake's work and only 7 miles from where her sister Jess lived with her partner Mo, who just happened to be Jake's newly promoted DI. 'Life is good,' she thought, as she touched her burgeoning belly that was home to their 4-month-old foetus.

The house was perfect and set in an acre of beautiful landscaped gardens. Both she and Jake liked the clean lines of the new build, unlike Jess who preferred her 19th Century country cottage. The house had a large kitchen /breakfast room, separate dining room and a large double-aspect sitting room that had French doors opening into an octagonal shaped conservatory. The four bedrooms were all doubles; the master, theirs, had an en suite shower room and walk in wardrobe. The large family bathroom completed the upstairs layout.

She had never been happier, at 34 she had it all; a handsome attentive husband who she loved, their first child on the way, she was a successful author (Crime Fiction) and this beautiful home. She sighed contentedly and headed for the shower.

6

Zoe cursed and ran downstairs hoping to get to the door before the bell rang again and woke Zak. Not expecting anyone she put the security chain in place before opening the door. Surprised and annoyed to see him standing on her doorstep, she said "what the hell are you doing here?"

"Candy baby or should I say Zoe, is that anyway to talk to the best client you've ever had? I come bearing gifts," he said, holding up a decent bottle of red wine. "So let me in and we can get on with being friendly again."

"I don't see clients at home and, more to the point, how the hell did you know where I lived?"

"Simple, I waited outside the club one night and followed you."

"Well you had a wasted journey then. As I said before, I don't see clients at home."

"But you'll see this one unless you want your classy neighbours to know what you do for a living."

"Are you threatening me?"

"No, just telling it as it is. Be nice and there'll be no need for any unpleasantness. Just let me in, give me a good time and I'll leave. Where's the harm?"

Feeling trapped Zoe took off the chain and opened the door.

"This is the first and last time you turn up here, right? In future I'm only available at the club, are we understood?"

"Loud and clear," he said, pushing past her into the hallway.

She looked around, happy that no one had seen him arrive, she closed the door behind him.

"Down there on the left," she said, pointing him in the direction of the sitting room.

"Wouldn't we be more comfortable upstairs?"

"My son's asleep upstairs, I prefer to stay down here."

"Don't be difficult Zoe, I want to go upstairs. It's irrelevant to me who else is up there. So unless you want me to wake him up and make him watch, I suggest we go up there now."

She was shocked by the malice in his voice and the meanness in those pale blue eyes. At the club he'd always seemed mild mannered and grateful. She felt a shiver of apprehension run down her spine.

"Nice house," he commented, as they climbed the stairs. On the landing she ushered him into her bedroom, the largest of the three on the second floor. He sat down on the edge of the king size bed and smiled.

"Now be a poppet and bring up a couple of glasses so we can enjoy a drink together first."

"I don't want a drink, dammit, let's just get on with it shall we?" she said, as she began unbuttoning her blouse.

"Zoe, such impatience! Anyone would think you didn't want me here."

"I don't, I didn't invite you and I don't take kindly to threats. But you won't go without a fuss until you get what you came for and, for what it's worth, I drink with friends not clients in my own home."

"Zoe, you're a whore, you get paid for sex. You take my money, you do my bidding."

"I don't want your money, I just want you to leave."

"Not an option," he snarled. Standing up, he grabbed her round the waist and pushed her towards the bed.

"You don't want to be nice? Well I can play that game too." And then he slapped her, so hard that she fell backwards onto the bed.

She stifled a scream, terrified that she would wake Zak. What was happening here, he'd never been violent before; it was as if his personality had changed overnight. Rubbing her reddened cheek she looked up at him and simply asked "Why are you doing this?"

"Because I can, now I know who I am and where the whores in my life belong."

"Where?"

"In hell."

Now she was really scared, she tried to sit up but suddenly he was astride her, hands around her throat, fingers digging in making it hard for her to breathe. Zoe fought hard, kicking and punching but slowly losing the battle as she slipped into unconsciousness. He just kept on squeezing until he was sure she was dead.

Smiling he stood over her body, pulled a condom from his trouser pocket, unzipped his fly and jerked off. After gratification he tied up the condom, stuffed it back into his pocket and looking down at her lifeless form said "essential housekeeping Zoe, you're just the first on my to do list so I mustn't leave any clues behind."

Suddenly he heard the creak of the bedroom door opening and turning towards it saw a small boy standing in the doorway rubbing his eyes.

Still half asleep he muttered "Mummy, I need a drink."

He swung the child up into his arms and carrying him out of the room said "mummy has a headache, she's asleep. I'll get you a glass of water."

Looking worried the boy asked, "who are you?"

"Your worst nightmare," he answered, as he broke the boy's fragile neck.

"You should have stayed in bed."

***

I felt bad about the boy, he should've stayed asleep. I couldn't leave him alive to identify me now could I? It was probably for the best though; motherless kids often end up in care don't they? I laid his body on the bed beside his mother. I left 22 Birchfield Avenue through the patio doors two hours later, satisfied that no trace of me ever having been there remained. The house backed onto a tree-lined footpath that ran beside open fields so there was much less chance of being seen as I made my way back to my car parked on Drakes Avenue, a good 400-yards away.

7

Cora Allen put down the phone and sighed. Had she done the right thing, phoning Connolly? They'd met when she moved down from Manchester; Connolly was a young beat cop then, who just happened to patrol the area round Fenton Street where the club was located. Although initially against the idea of a club like the Blue Lagoon operating in her town, Mo soon realised that Cora, an astute business woman, was running an upper class establishment that provided a service, albeit a service that Mo neither liked nor agreed with. Cora ran a tight ship and never had reason to call the police to the club; most of the clients were well heeled business men and just didn't cause trouble, only there for a good night out and uncomplicated sex. If the odd stag party got a bit rowdy Nick and the doormen were more than capable of dealing with it. Despite Mo's early misgivings, a mutual respect had grown between the two women and when she transferred to CID she still dropped in for the occasional drink and catch up. Cora would never call a cop a friend, but Mo Connolly came close.

Zoe wouldn't be happy about the police calling round but Cora was feeling anxious about her. She knew that Zoe's sister Diana had taken the family to Cornwall for a week, so there was no one else around who gave a damn. The fact that the normally reliable Zoe hadn't even bothered to phone in gave Cora cause for concern, so much so that last night she'd sent Nick Danvers round to the house to check on her. A fruitless task because he couldn't get anyone to answer the door despite the upstairs curtains being drawn and the lights on. Cora had a restless night and, sensing something was really wrong, this morning she'd called Connolly on impulse. She was confident that Mo would take a look and, moreover, keep it discreet and not involve uniformed officers.

She paced the apartment like a caged lioness worried about one of her cubs. She'd liked Zoe from the moment they'd met, almost three years ago. The pretty twenty-four-year-old had applied for job waiting tables in the restaurant. She'd appeared nervous at interview and Cora learned later that she was overwhelmed by the sheer grandeur of the club and didn't think she had a hope in hell of getting the job. She hadn't worked before, had no experience of waitressing but nonetheless there was something about the girl, a certain naiveté and honesty that impressed Cora and she decided to give the girl a chance. The right decision, Zoe was quick to learn and within a week was matching the skills of the more seasoned staff.

Cora took an interest in all of her employees and was soon aware of the circumstances that led Zoe to her door. The disastrous affair, the pregnancy, the determination to give her son a decent life, all this and a strong work ethic gained Cora's admiration. She was surprised when six months later Zoe asked if there was any chance of becoming a club hostess. She was an intelligent woman, she must know the score but Cora just couldn't picture Zoe in the role of 'working girl'.

"Come in early tomorrow, come up to the apartment and we'll talk then," she said, wondering if she could talk Zoe out of the life that she'd so readily embraced all those years ago.

The next night Zoe arrived at the apartment around 6:30pm.

"So you want to be a hostess? You do know what the job entails?" Cora asked, raising her eyebrows and giving Zoe a searching look.

"Of course."

"Then why on earth would a decent girl like you want to do it?"

"I need the money. I want to be independent, a house of my own, a decent place to raise Zak. The job in the restaurant pays well and the tips are good but it's just not enough to get myself on the property ladder and away from the constant demands of my sister's family. I need my own space and this job would give me the opportunity to have it."

"You're an intelligent girl Zoe, you could do anything."

"College dropout, no meaningful qualifications for a high flying career, where exactly could I get a salary paying the sort of money your girls can earn?"

"Okay you have a point but are you sure it's what you want?"

"It's what I need to give me the lifestyle I want. I don't intend to do it forever, only 'til I can get my old life back, work my way through college and get a well-paid career out there in the real world. Until then I'll just close my eyes and count the money, cynical I know but, please Cora, give me this opportunity to make good."

So Cora did and Zoe prospered financially.

The office phone rang interrupting her memories and filling her with trepidation.

"Cora, its Mo Connolly."

8

DC John Jackson, Jacko to his mates, was Newbury Station's resident computer nerd. He scratched the stubble on his square jaw, deep in thought. He'd been working on this case for three days without a hint of a breakthrough. Counterfeit pound coins were appearing regularly in the community; the police had heard a whisper that local, fly by night, businessman Reggie Prentiss may well be involved in their distribution and Jacko was trying to establish any link between Prentiss and the North London villains suspected of producing them. The Met had their eye on one fellow in particular, a Jeff Ironside, drug dealer, strip club owner and one time enforcer for Tony Drake. Drake being one of North London's criminal elite. If there was a link Jacko couldn't find it and maybe the information was just that, a whisper from a bloke with a grudge. He looked up and saw the DCI going into his office; unhappy to admit defeat he thought he should at least share his frustration with Jake Summers. He got up went over to Jake's office and knocked.

"Come in."

Jacko opened the door.

"About Reggie Prentiss Guv."

Jake could tell from his slumped shoulders that Jacko hadn't found anything to incriminate Prentiss.

"No luck then Jacko?"

"Not so far Guv, how reliable is the witness?"

"Not sure, the whisper came via DS Miller and he was pretty convinced his source was legit so I guessed it was worth spending some time on."

"Do you want me to keep looking?"

"Give it another 24-hours and if you don't get a break just put it on the back burner, we may get more concrete evidence at some point."

Jacko looked disappointed about continuing with what he thought of as a thankless task.

"Think how impressed the Met will be if we do get a lead," Jake said.

"Not as impressed as I'll be," Jacko said, closing the office door behind him as he left.

Jake smiled. Jacko was a good bloke, a dogged researcher who usually came up with the goods. He really didn't like being beaten and if he was, he just wanted to throw in the towel and move on. Jake understood the principal of flogging a dead horse but Miller had sounded so sure about the information being reliable, devoting another 24-hours was worth it in Jake's eyes. If they could nab Prentiss it would be a real coup. Well known to the police, and as slippery as an eel, the bastard had always managed to avoid prosecution.

Things were quiet in the department at the moment; DS Dusty Miller and DC Steve Halliday were working an aggravated assault and robbery case. The victim, a nineteen-year-old man, had been robbed at knife point outside the Ruddy Duck Public House on Saturday night. He'd suffered stab wounds to both arms, nothing life threatening but in need of stitches. The attacker had stolen his mobile phone and a wallet containing £55. This was the third such attack in as many weeks and Jake wanted the culprit caught quickly before someone was killed. Recently promoted Miller was leading the investigation and Jake trusted him and the super keen Halliday to give it their best shot and hopefully wrap it up quickly. He got up and opened the door just as Miller was about to knock.

"I was just thinking about your case Alan, how's it going?"

"I think we've got him Guv. Adrian Hewitt attempted to rob thirty-five-year-old Jay Butler, a sergeant in the Royal Marines no less. Big mistake. Hewitt was disarmed in seconds and then Butler phoned us on his mobile. He's holding the unwashed longhaired scally, his description not mine, at the Panini Sandwich Bar on Chively Road so we're on our way there now."

"Result, what a div picking on a Marine."

"To be fair Guv, the bloke wasn't in uniform."

"Our good fortune then, he just picked on the wrong guy to rob. Go bring him in Alan and well done."

"Just a lucky break Guv."

"They all count."

Jake watched as Miller and Halliday left the department and thought 'then there were two'. Jacko tucked away in the corner with his computer and DC Rhona Grey, recently transferred from the Serious Crime Unit at Thames Valley Police Headquarters in Oxford. Born in Glasgow she was an attractive 28-year-old brunette. She was engaged to a local GP, the reason for the transfer, had a degree in Criminology and Psychology from UWE in Bristol and was proving to be a very useful addition to the squad. Jake walked over to her desk. She was busy reading a case file but looked up immediately

"Sir?"

"Didn't mean to interrupt Rhona, just wondering what you're working on."

"It's a case uniform passed upstairs; a hit and run in Welford, happened Wednesday last week. The victim, a Christine Jamieson, was found dead at the scene. Yesterday a witness, Joanna Nickerson, came forward out of the blue, said she'd seen a silver grey car mount the pavement, deliberately target Jamieson and then drive off at speed. So it appears it's no longer a simple hit and run case. Inspector Leyland passed it on to DI Connolly who asked me to take a fresh look at the file and then go and question Joanna Nickerson myself."

"Did she get a number?"

"Partial sir, RK or RR 51 or 61 are as good as it gets. She's sure about the first letter being R and the number 1 but the others are iffy and she didn't get any of the last 3 identification letters. She thought the car looked newish so I'm plumping for 61, which makes it a local 2011 registration."

"Sounds as if you're already hot on the trail?"

"Well it's a start, Sir"

"What took her so long to come forward?"

"Because, believe it or not, she didn't want to get involved but then her conscience kicked in when she saw the police appeal for witnesses. You just can't predict how people will react in any given situation can you Sir?"

"Unfortunately no, it would make our job so much easier if you could. Just one other thing Rhona."

"Sir?"

"We're pretty informal here so call me Guv eh?"

The phone in Jake's office rang.

"Right, I need to get that so I'll leave you in peace with your hit and run, it's obviously in good hands."

He picked up the phone.

"Summers."

"Guv, it's me," Mo said, in a shaky voice..

9

Mo and Dave Gregg arrived outside The Dryden residence at 8:32 am. Mo had briefed him on the way.

"Not an official investigation Dave, just doing a favour for Cora Allen. She's worried about one of her girls, Zoe Dryden. She hasn't been seen at the club for three days, hasn't been in contact and, according to Cora, that's unheard of and gives her cause for concern. So if she's home fine, we'll just tell her to get in touch. If she's not, then we'll have to think again."

Gregg climbed out of the car and whistled.

"Nice Mickey Mouse Guv, she must make plenty of Duane Eddies being one of Cora's Brass Doors."

"Translated means?" Mo snapped, frustrated as always by Gregg's use of cockney slang, especially this early in the day.

"Sorree Guv, nice house she must make good money working as a prostitute."

"Better, try and remember we're not all Cockneys in the squad Dave." She knew he wouldn't they'd had this conversation countless times before.

She'd already clocked the lights and the drawn curtains upstairs as she rang the doorbell. They waited on the doorstep for a couple of minutes, no answer.

"No one home then Guv, back to the station yes?"

"I don't like it Dave, lights on upstairs, curtains drawn. Why would anyone leave the house without turning the lights off, eh?"

"People do, I'm always telling my old lady to switch 'em off."

"Maybe, but I have a bad feeling about this one. Go round back and see if you can see anything. I'll ring again, she could always be in the shower or something."

Mo watched as Gregg went through the side gate to the back garden, she rang the bell again, still no answer. Gregg was back within minutes.

"Anything?"

"Nothing much to see downstairs, no sign of life in the lounge or kitchen, kitchen door is locked but the patio door isn't. It's a sliding door, it's closed but not locked. Are we going in?"

"Call from a concerned employer, lights on upstairs, property not secured. Probable cause?"

"Probable cause Guv."

Happy they were singing from the same hymn sheet, Mo led the way to the back of the house slid open the patio door and went inside. The room was large and airy, nothing obviously out of place just like Gregg said 'nothing to see'. She crossed to the door, opened it and went into the hallway. They checked the other downstairs rooms, nothing.

"Let's take a look upstairs, Dave."

The square landing had closed doors on all sides. The first one Mo opened was obviously the kid's room. One feature wall was covered with a lunar landing site complete with space suited men and a ship that looked much like Captain Kirk's Starship Enterprise. The single bed was unmade and the sheets rumpled as if someone had just climbed out of them. The night light on the bedside table was on. Mo's heart sank; surely no mother would go out leave the house in this state. Gregg had already opened the door opposite and found the family bathroom.

"Nothing here Guv, perhaps they've done a moonlight."

"Gut feeling says not."

She moved to the next door and opened it, and then the unmistakable smell of decomposing flesh hit her like a blow to the solar plexus and made her gag. Her hand flew up to her nose and, quickly pinching her nostrils shut with finger and thumb, she glanced over to the bed. Her worst fears were confirmed; two bodies posed to look like they were sleeping. The boys head on his mother's shoulder, her arm encircling his small body, holding him close. She felt a tear trickle down her face as she approached the bed. A few bluebottles, disturbed by her approach, rose into the air as one, buzzing and creating a macabre dance above the bodies. Sickened further by the disgusting insects she rushed into the bathroom and vomited her breakfast into the loo. Embarrassed by her lack of control, she looked up to see Gregg standing in the doorway.

"You okay Guv?" he asked, looking concerned.

Quickly flushing the loo she murmured, "fine thanks Dave. The smell was bad enough, seeing the kid made it worse and then the bloody flies tipped me over the edge. Sorry about that."

"No worries, I just closed the door on the poor buggers otherwise both of us would be hanging over the loo."

She went to the sink, turned on the tap and swilled her face with the cool water. Feeling better and regaining some composure she turned to Gregg.

"Mike Long won't be pleased with us tramping all over his crime scene, I'd better phone in."

Inspector Mike Long, a blunt talking Yorkshire man with intelligent blue eyes and a salt and pepper buzz cut, was the senior Scene of Crime Officer (SOCO) at Newbury. One of only a few police officers holding the post, mainly a civilian one, he was responsible for preserving forensic, photographic and fingerprint evidence from crime scenes and accidents. Mo took out her mobile and rang Long preparing herself for the bollocking that would follow the phone call.

She wasn't disappointed, he was furious even though she tried to explain that they had no reason to call him in before entering the house. Unappeased he said "stay put, don't touch anything else, I'll phone Freddie Saunders and be there in ten."

Looking at Dave Gregg she just shrugged.

"He's mad then?"

"Yeah, he's mad. I just hope by the time he gets here he's calmed down and realised that without us coming in there would be no crime scene to investigate. He's getting in touch with the pathologist too. I'd better call DCI Summers and put him in the picture." They went back downstairs and waited.

10

JEB CARTER

Henry King couldn't believe that Olivia had just upped and left him with no explanation and I was sick to death of hearing his bleating and tearful "we were happy Jeb; I know we were happy, why did she leave me?"

And my reply as always was "because she's a woman Henry and I challenge any man to understand why they do what they do. Look at my Ginny, she ran off with that fucking wimp of a school teacher, not satisfied with the real man she already had at home."

The village bobby, Jeremiah Lamplugh, was less than interested when Ginny disappeared. Having heard the rumours, like everyone else, he was convinced she'd run off with Simmons but Olivia King was a different kettle of fish. Lamplugh, sweet on Olivia himself before Henry came along, was like a dog with a bone; not satisfied that she'd just packed her bags and left he called in senior officers from Northallerton, the recently built headquarters of the North Riding constabulary. They suspected foul play and Henry was their number one suspect, but without a body they had no proof a crime had ever been committed. I prided myself on a job well done and Lamplugh was left to cast suspicious looks in Henry's direction every time he clapped eyes on him.

I, on the other hand, free from any suspicion was ready to embark upon another adventure with the delightful Esme Hawkins. She came from Heath Overton, a village two miles west of Stanton and was walking out with the local Blacksmith Benjamin Raines. Raines, a widower in his mid-thirties, was no doubt considered a good catch; with his own business and the nice little house he owned in Stanton. He had no children to complicate their future together, his wife had died in childbirth and the premature baby had followed a week later. To Esme, at least 12-years his junior, a pretty little thing with blonde curls and a cute smile, he must seem an attractive proposition. He wasn't a handsome man but he had the means to give her a comfortable lifestyle. She worked in the kitchen at Glebe Farm. I'd spotted her there a few times, seen her in the village when she was out walking with Raines and had been impressed by her girlish good looks. Now after weeks of fantasising about her I felt it was time to introduce myself. Every Tuesday, her day off, she went back to visit family in Heath Overton. She left the farm early, around 7:30am. If the weather was fine she walked over the fields and took the canal path into Heath Overton cutting almost a mile from the journey by road. In the evening her father brought her back in his buggy.

It was Tuesday, it was 7:30am, it was a beautiful day and a few wispy clouds peppered the blue sky. I waited patiently by the gate in Coxwell Meadow. I had my scythe with me, ready to explain that I'd been sent there by Monkman to cut the long grass. In truth I should be clearing ditches half a mile away but I would get to that later. It would be done by the time Monkman did his weekly check on Friday even if it meant working late into the evening. He'd never thought of me as family although I'd been married to his granddaughter and now with her gone I was just another farmhand. He let me keep the cottage but was always hinting that they should only be occupied by families. He's just waiting for any excuse to sack me and turf me off Glebe Farm and out of their swanky lives for good.

I see her in the distance and busy myself by the gate, watching from the corner of my eye as she approaches. She unlatches the gate and enters the meadow behind me. I look up and smile. Taking the cap from my head and wiping the sweat from my brow, I greet her.

"Good morning, lovely day for a stroll."

She's dressed in her Sunday best, straw hat hiding most of her blonde curls, a neatly pressed white blouse tucked into an ankle length brown skirt and tan leather woven lace up brogues. She looks at me coyly and I see the first flicker of recognition in her eyes.

"You're Jeb, Mr Monkman's grandson aren't you? I've seen you at the house."

"Grandson? I suppose so, in a manner of speaking. I was married to Ginny, his granddaughter. Counts for nothing though, today I'm a merely a farmhand responsible for cutting down the long grass," I reply, swinging the scythe in front of me.

"That looks like hard work on your own. Is anyone coming to help?"

"Not unless he's sent you," I say, teasing her.

"'Fraid not, it's my day off. I'm going to Heath Overton to visit my folks."

"Not today, today you'll be pleasuring me," I say, throwing down the scythe and grabbing her round the waist.

My body responds quickly to the feel of her struggling against me. I swing her off her feet and push her down into the long grass. Straddling her body I hold her captive with my muscular legs. I look down at her expecting to see fear in her eyes, but there is no fear only defiance.

"Get off me Jeb Carter before my dad gets here. He comes to meet me every Tuesday and I swear he'll knock your block off if he catches you messing with me."

Smiling at her false display of courage I simply say "fibber" and begin to tear at clothing.

The realisation that I know no one is coming to help her brings fear into those defiant blue eyes and she starts to scream. I slap her hard, leaving the imprint of my hand on her pale cheek; she stops screaming and begins to sob.

"Better, make it easy on yourself, defiance brings out the worst in me," and then I hit her again to re-enforce my message. Dazed but still conscious she stops struggling the rest is easy. I rip open her blouse, pull up the chemise beneath it and knead her small white breast pinching the nipple between my thumb and forefinger. With my free hand I lift her skirt and petticoat, she isn't wearing a corset, just pretty white calf length drawers. Releasing her breast I use both hands to pull them down to her ankles exposing the triangle of golden hair that covers her sex. Still sitting astride her I push down my braces and pull down my pants allowing my swollen cock to spring free. Slipping my hands under her hips I arch her body upwards allowing me to enter her. She's wide awake now and screaming with pain as I move inside her, destroying the last barrier of her innocence. Her screams just make me thrust harder until I explode inside her. She has passed out with the pain and lies still on the flattened grass, blood stains the inside of her thighs and I feel nothing but satisfaction knowing that I am the first and last man to have her. I put my hands around her throat and end her short life. I dress, remove the small silver locket from round her neck, drop it into my pocket. A souvenir to remember her by. I'll bury her next to Livie in Anderley Wood.

11

Jake listened in silence as Mo reported the details of what she'd found at the house in Birchfield Avenue.

"The killer positioned the bodies to look as if the child was sleeping in his mother's arms but the smell and the presence of those disgusting insects told me otherwise. It was truly awful Guv."

Despite feeling saddened by her distress he had to smile when she said "I phoned Mike and he's as mad as hell, cos according to him we had no right going in and trashing his crime scene."

"You know Mike Mo, he'll calm down and if he doesn't I'm on my way to smooth things over. You did the right thing, trust me. I'll bring young Grey with me and she and Gregg can start knocking on doors, find out if the neighbours have seen anyone hanging around. And Mo, give Cora Allen a ring, tell her the situation as it stands and let her know someone will be round later to question her."

"I'll go myself when we're done here. She knows me from way back and will talk more freely to someone she's comfortable with. We had a rocky start but we worked through that and now we do have a certain amount of respect for each other. I know what you're thinking, the cop and the madam hardly a match made in heaven but it works okay?"

Jake laughed glad to hear her sounding more like the animated Mo he knew.

"Does Jess know about Cora and this match made in heaven?" he teased.

"Ha bloody ha," she said, laughing herself. "See you soon Guv," and she ended the call.

Twenty minutes later Jake and Rhona arrived at Birchfield Avenue. The house concerned was made conspicuous by the presence of aluminum barriers linked by yellow crime scene tape surrounding it and the young uniformed PC stationed at the front gate. Jake didn't recognise him so fished out his warrant card.

"DCI Summers and DC Grey, we need to get inside lad."

The young PC took out his notebook and logged their names.

Jake had already noticed that the unusual presence of police here had attracted the twitching curtain brigade and, even more conspicuously, 'the neighbourhood watch' were out in force standing in open doorways, monitoring the situation and doubtless drawing their own conclusions. People were so predictable, if they don't know what's happening they indulge in speculation.

"Inspector Long has asked that officers enter by the patio doors round back Sir. Apparently that entrance has already been violated."

Jake smiled at the young cop's description. "Then that's where we're heading, wouldn't want to violate another entrance now would we?" he said, nodding to Grey to follow him."

He peered through the glass and signalled to the booted and suited detectives inside. Mo slid open the door and let them in but only after they'd donned the white suits, gloves and boots that were a necessary requirement when attending a crime scene.

"I know why we're expected to wear these togs but why you two? You've already trashed the scene," Jake said grinning.

"Too bloody right," Mike Long said, as he came into the room. "Not one but two sets of size tens trampling over the evidence. Not funny Sir, makes our job so much harder. I told them to suit up so they don't create more havoc but it's probably too little too late."

"Don't be too hard on them Mike, they just came here for a look see after a phone call from an anxious employer. They didn't know they were entering a crime scene, I'd have done exactly the same thing."

Mike looked at him raised one bushy eyebrow and said "You would? Really?"

"Yeah I would."

"Then it's just as well you didn't come with them Sir, otherwise there'd be three sets of size tens to worry about," he replied, clapping Jake on the back and grinning. Jake looked over to Mo and winked.

"So they're forgiven then?"

"Only because my techies tell me the place looks like it's been wiped clean. The only prints they can find are fresh and probably belong to Beavis and Butthead there," he said, nodding towards Connolly and Gregg.

"So what have you found?"

"Not too much I'm afraid. No forced entry, she either let him in or he gained access through the patio doors which DI Connolly tells me were left open. My best guess is she knew her killer, let him in because she didn't feel threatened, and then after the deed he exited through the garden leaving the patio doors unlocked behind him. Freddie's upstairs now if you want a word before he has the bodies moved to the morgue. It's not pleasant up there, the smell's bad enough but seeing the young kid and his mother like that is heart-breaking. Why would anyone kill a young kid?"

Jake could detect the sadness in the voice of the normally blunt talking, no nonsense Yorkshireman, who had three boys of his own.

"Because, unfortunately, there'll always be monsters out there Mike. All we can do is catch them before they ruin more lives. I'll go up and see Freddie, maybe he can tell us something that will help us put this bastard behind bars. Coming Mo?"

"I'll pass thanks, I lost my breakfast first time round and I'm not anxious to embarrass myself again."

"Yeah it's pretty bad up there Guv, I nearly peppered the porcelain too," Gregg added, grinning.

Jake noticed Rhona Grey wrinkle her nose and said "too much information Dave. Okay I'll go talk to Freddie, you three wait here and Mo, don't feel embarrassed we've all been there."

Jake left the room with Mike Long hot on his heels. Moments later Mo heard their animated voices drifting downstairs. The three of them waited in silence until Jake re-joined them in the lounge.

"Looks as if Zoe Dryden was strangled and her son had his neck broken. Zoe Dryden's still fully clothed, the boy's wearing pyjamas so the motive probably not a sexual one but we won't know anything for sure until the autopsy is complete. Freddie Saunders estimates time of death 72-84 hours ago. So Rhona, Dave get out there and talk to neighbours, find out if anyone knows anything. Judging by what's happening now they're a nosey bunch so just maybe someone saw something. Mo, let's pay Cora Allen a visit."

12

JEB CARTER

They've arrested Henry King for the murders of his wife Olivia and another female victim. It's all folk can talk about in the Taverner's Arms tonight. Apparently two days ago Seth Morgan was rabbiting in Anderley Woods with his brother Matt and their Border Terrier crossbreed. The dog partially unearthed Olivia's body. The police were called, they dug up the body, found the clothes I'd buried with her and from that were able to identify Olivia. Further excavation revealed another body buried about 5-yards from the first which they assume to be the missing Esme Hawkins. Her parents have been called in to see if they can identify her remains and the clothing she was wearing. Henry, always Jeremiah Lamplugh's prime suspect, was arrested and is now awaiting trial in Northallerton. Of course, according to 'I told you so' Lamplugh, they had to drag him away kicking and screaming protesting his innocence. But then the poor sod would, after all he is innocent. Sorry mate, I didn't expect the bodies to be found but then I hadn't counted on the Morgan brothers and their bloody dog. Of course now they have been it makes things difficult for me. No more local lasses can disappear, not with Henry locked up otherwise the Bobbies will start looking elsewhere for the killer and that's the last think I need. Henry's cousin, Ed Tierney, is at the bar now telling everyone who'll listen that Henry would never hurt a fly and the police have got it all wrong. Henry was popular here and several men are nodding their heads in agreement.

Having heard enough I pick up my jacket and prepare to leave when the barmaid Mary Tindal leans over the bar and shouts "leaving us already Jeb? You've only had one glass surely you have time for another?"

I walk over and put my empty glass on the counter.

"Not tonight Mary, tonight I'm off home."

"Course Henry was a friend of yours wasn't he? We all liked him at the Taverners, never thought he was capable of murder."

"Yeah he was a friend and for the record, I don't believe he killed anyone."

She leans forward thrusting her ample breasts in my direction and whispers "me neither, and if I can put a smile back on your face I'd be happy to try when I finish up here."

As she leans in close I can smell the sourness of her breath and I quickly take a step back to escape the assault on my senses.

"Are you flirting with me Mary Tindal?" I ask, studying her and not really liking what I see. A buxom redhead, her pale face etched with fine lines making her look much older than her thirty-five years. Tonight she's making it pretty clear she has me in her sights even though her old fella is sitting in the corner slouched over an empty glass.

"What about Tom?" I ask, nodding towards the corner.

"Just buy him another drink and he won't give a damn." She smiles, exposing a mouthful of rotten teeth.

"But I will slut," I hiss through clenched teeth wishing Henry were still free and I could rid the world of this ugly trollop.

"Piss off home then you miserable sod. It's no wonder your Ginny ran off with the school teacher."

I manage to walk away even though every fibre of my being wants to strangle the life from her. Strolling home I consider my options:

1.   I need a woman to fulfill my physical needs.

2.   I'm poor; divorce (although not necessary now I know my wife is dead, though no one else suspects it) is not an option so I can't offer marriage.

3.   I'm still young, fit and reasonably handsome so it shouldn't be difficult to persuade some hapless girl to share my miserable existence.

4.   If my urge to kill becomes overpowering, and it will, I'll just look for victims further afield.

All is not lost. I have a plan of action.

13

Mo rang the bell outside the Blue Lagoon and Nick Danvers let them in.

"Is Cora expecting you?" he asked Mo while giving Jake a suspicious once over.

"I phoned earlier, Nick. This is DCI Summers. I'm afraid we're here on official business."

"I'll give her buzz then, let her know you've arrived."

"Before you do Nick, did you see anyone hanging about when you went to Zoe Dryden's house last night?"

"No one, the street was deserted except for a few parked cars. I couldn't get an answer from Zoe either."

"Okay thanks, we may need to talk to you again later."

"Why? Has something happened to Zoe?"

"We'll talk later, now can you give Cora that buzz?"

Looking puzzled he walked over to the bar and picked up the internal phone. Mo could hear him explaining they were there and saying it seemed to be about Zoe.

Mo had been evasive when she'd phoned earlier, just telling Cora she needed to speak to her.

Nick came back over and told them to take the lift up to Cora's apartment on the 2nd floor.

Once they were in the lift Jake let out a low whistle and said "some place she must be loaded."

"Yeah, apparently she made some old guy really happy so he left her a wodge of money in his will allowing her to move from Manchester and buy this little goldmine."

"I'm impressed, for a bordello it's a pretty classy establishment. She must have made him ecstatic to afford this."

"It's more like a gentleman's club, complete with restaurant providing fine wines and fine dining. Clients need to be wealthy to eat and drink here and even better off to afford one of the working girls. She offered me a job once," Mo laughed, "but that's another story."

The lift stopped and opened into a narrow hallway. Cora was standing at the open doorway opposite and beckoned them over. Jake had heard about the woman but never met her and hadn't known what to expect. It certainly wasn't the tall elegant grey-haired woman that greeted them. Mo made the introductions and they followed Cora through the apartment into a large airy sitting room.

"Have a seat," she said, pointing to one of the two black leather sofas on either side of a large oak coffee table. "Can I get you a drink?"

"Coffee please," said Mo, hoping it would settle the queasy feeling still in the pit of her stomach.

"Nothing for me thanks," Jake answered politely.

"Not at all what I expected," he whispered, as Cora left the room.

Mo smiled and winked "not the dumpy brass haired tart you'd expect to run a brothel then?"

"Definitely not, more the lady of the manor type."

"Cora may run a brothel but she's also a very astute business woman."

Before Jake could comment, Cora returned with two coffees. She handed one to Mo then sat down with hers on the sofa opposite.

Pleasantries over they told her what they'd found at Birchfield Avenue.

Cora Allen looked distraught. The news of the deaths of Zoe Dryden and her son Zak had hit her harder than she could imagine. She suspected something was wrong when Connolly phoned and asked if she could come over and have a chat, but knowing was infinitely worse. A single tear escaped from the corner of her eye and rolled down her left cheek.

Seeing her so visibly upset Mo was quick to rise, sit beside her, and put a comforting arm around her shoulders. That's when Cora really lost control and sobbed in Mo's arms. The unexpected reaction from this strong woman, normally in control of her emotions, left the detectives speechless.

All Mo could do was hold her until the crying finally subsided. Then looking up with puffy red rimmed eyes and a tear stained face Cora just murmured "sorry, we were close."

"I'm sorry too," Mo said, "if I'd known you were going to take it so badly I would've handled it differently.

Cora shook off Mo's comforting arm and moved away from her.

"But you didn't know, and besides if someone's been murdered how the hell do you tell it differently? Do you have any idea who did it?"

The tears had been replaced by anger and the anger was being directed at Mo.

"No we don't Ms Allen," Jake interrupted, "that's why we're here to ask if you know anyone that would harm Zoe and her son."

"If I'd had a daughter I'd want her to be just like Zoe and no, I can't imagine anyone wanting to kill her, everyone liked her. She worked here purely to afford the things she needed, a house, to finish college and then a career. She wasn't a whore, she just loved her son and wanted the best for him and herself."

"What about the boy's father? Is he still around?" Jake asked.

"No, the bastard hightailed it back to the Caribbean as soon as he found out she was pregnant. Her parents weren't any help either. The father gave her an ultimatum, to get rid or get out so she got out. She had some help from the sister that lives here with her family, but Zoe was treated more like an unpaid nanny having to look after the sister's kids. She found it suffocating and needed a place of her own. That's how she came to work here, first as a waitress and then as a hostess. As she said, she needed the money. I knew from the off she wouldn't be here forever and I was right wasn't I?" she said, looking tearful again.

"So where can we reach the sister?"

"Diana, she lives on Holderness Road on the North side of town but she's away at the moment. The whole family are holidaying in Cornwall somewhere."

"You don't know where in Cornwall?"

"No, I doubt even Zoe knew where, and if she did she can't tell."

"Do you know where the husband works? He might have mentioned where they were going to a colleague."

"All I know is he's some sort of Engineer, I've no idea where he works, I don't even know their bloody surname. Zoe just referred to them as Rob and Diana."

"If we can't locate the family we need someone else to formally identify the bodies Ms Allen. As you knew both Zoe and her son, would you be willing to do that?"

"You mean you're not even sure it's them?"

"As sure as we can be, but formal identification is essential and as soon as possible, if you're willing?"

"Not willing but I'll do it."

"Thank you. Feel free to bring someone with you, identifying a body, particularly the body of someone close, can be pretty traumatic."

"I didn't think for a minute it'd be a picnic, perhaps I'll ask Nick Danvers."

"Before you do, did Zoe have any regular clients?"

"A few, she was very popular."

"If you can give us a list of their names we'll have a word."

"We do have a list of her clients, we keep them for all our girls. But I doubt they leave their real names, too much to lose if the wife finds out. We insist they always pay cash so we don't have credit card details either, but you're welcome to the names for what they're worth."

Mo hadn't spoken since Cora shrugged her off so angrily but now felt impelled to say "we will catch him you know."

"I pray to God you will, she didn't deserve to die."

"None of them ever do Cora," Mo said, sympathetically.

14

"Post's arrived." Linda Benson shouted upstairs as she picked the mail off the front door mat.

"He's early today, we haven't even opened up yet," Kate said, as she came through the connecting door into the shop.

"Probably on a promise," Linda laughed, as she leafed through the mail. "Two for you, a letter and a returned package marked address unknown."

Kate took the letter and the padded envelope from Linda's outstretched hand.

The padded envelope contained the CD and notes from David Mitchell's past life regression.

"Strange, I remember this guy actually gave me a printed card with his name and address on. And yet it's been returned. I know I addressed it correctly, I remember checking carefully, him being my first paying client. It's that Mitchell fellow, remember I told you how weird he acted after the session?"

"Sort of, was he the guy who freaked you out and made you decide not to be in the building alone when you saw clients?"

"That's him."

"Why the false address I wonder?"

"I've no idea. He was certainly keen to be regressed but acted really weird after the session, almost as if he'd taken on the personality of his former incarnation, a Jeb Carter."

"Oh well, if he doesn't want it why worry, he paid you that's the important thing."

"I suppose." But Kate being Kate, she just couldn't let it drop and that evening her curiosity prompted her to do a search on her computer. She judged Mitchell to be mid to late thirties so typed in David Mitchell born c1977 in Newbury Berkshire and hit return.

There were several hits, mainly professional profiles on LinkedIn but the one that caught her interest was a newspaper report dated 19th March 2001. A 24-year-old man, victim of a hit and run, named David Mitchell. The father, a James Mitchell, was offering a reward of £10,000 for information leading to the arrest of the person guilty of killing his son. According to the article the Mitchell family lived at Patrick Close, Newbury, Berkshire. Her eyes widened, Patrick Close surely that's where her David Mitchell lived and that's where she'd sent the package. She rooted through the business cards in the top drawer of her desk and there it was.

David Mitchell
25 Patrick Close
Newbury
Berkshire

But it can't be the same David Mitchell, he'd be the right age at 37 but if the news report was accurate, he'd died 13-years ago.

Puzzled, Kate typed in Patrick Close Newbury.

Another headline.

Newbury, 2nd August 2006

Despite fierce opposition, residents of Patrick Close and the adjoining Rookham Crescent were today served with compulsory purchase orders on their properties. The houses are to be demolished to make way for a new library and council offices. Building is due to start in May 2007.

"Oh my God. I've given past life regression to a dead man," she exclaimed, feeling a chill run down her spine. But she knew in reality that the David Mitchell she knew was very much alive and if he'd given a false name and address he probably had something to hide. She was worried now, what did he have to hide? Was he dangerous, would he be back because she could recognise him? A clap of thunder made her jump and she screamed hysterically then, taking a deep breath and regaining her composure, muttered "you're being paranoid Kate, get a grip."

She still felt uneasy though and felt she had to share her unease with someone. Her first thought was Linda, she would ring Linda but perhaps that wasn't such a good idea because she knew what Linda would say "you're being paranoid Kate get a grip." That at least made her smile and then it came to her, tomorrow she'd ring Jaime Summers.

Kate knew her sister Jess Mason quite well; they both went to Linda's meditation group meetings on the first Wednesday of the month. Several weeks ago Jess asked if Kate would be willing to talk to Jaime about past life regression, apparently the novelist wanted to incorporate it into the plot of a new book she was planning to write. Kate was flattered and willingly agreed. She'd liked Jaime immediately, very different from Jess but equally engaging. A crime writer married to a detective, yes the very person Kate needed to speak to.

15

Cora looked down at the lifeless face of Zoe Dryden then looked towards Mo Connolly and nodded.

"Yes, God help us it's Zoe."

She turned to Nick Danvers and buried her head in his shoulder. His pale face looked grim as he encircled her with a comforting arm. Jake stepped forward.

"I'm sorry to ask but would you take a look at the boy's body now?"

"I'll do it," Danvers said, "I think Cora's had enough heartache for one day."

"Thanks Nick," Mo said, taking Cora's elbow and leading her away.

"That him, poor little blighter, that's Zak Dryden," Danvers confirmed. "What kind of sick bastard kills a child?"

"A very sick bastard and we need to put him where he belongs behind bars, as soon as possible," Jake replied.

"Six feet under would be my preferred option," Nick hissed, his face contorted with anger.

Not expecting such an impassioned outburst, Jake turned towards him. His eyes had glazed over, his hands were clenched so tightly together that the knuckles had turned white and his face was deathly pale. Jake, realising that Danvers was in shock and about to keel over, took hold of his arm and said "let's get you out of here."

Those few words were enough to bring Nick Danvers back from the brink and out of his stupor.

"Yes sounds good, let's get out of here," he said gruffly.

Jake nodded to the Mortuary assistant. "Thanks Simon, we're done here now," and still holding onto Danvers arm left the room. In the corridor outside it was decided that Mo would drive Danvers and Cora Allen back to the club and Jake would walk back to the Station.

As he was about to leave Freddie Saunders tapped him on the shoulder.

"A word before you go." He ushered Jake into his office closing the door firmly behind them. Saunders was a stocky, sharp featured, balding and bespectacled fellow and looked more like a history professor than a forensic pathologist, but Jake knew that those keen blue eyes didn't miss a thing and, moreover, he was a good guy to work with.

"I didn't want to say anything in front of the relatives."

"They're work colleagues not relatives."

"Even more reason then, you'll probably want to keep this under wraps anyway."

"Spit it out Freddie and I'll tell you if it needs suppressing."

"He stitched her up, the bastard stitched her up."

"Stitched her up, I'm not understanding you Freddie."

"I did a preliminary external exam this morning, removed clothing and found that Zoe Dryden's outer labia had been sutured together, effectively closing off the vaginal entrance. It was done post mortem and with very little finesse so I doubt the killer has any surgical experience. He used a running suture, not individual stitches and from the size of the needle holes and the type of thread, I'd say he probably used an emergency survival suture kit or the like. "

"Give that to me in layman's terms."

"Okay, imagine you have an open wound on your arm. To close that wound we need to draw the two sides together. This is done by inserting the needle one side of the wound then pulling the thread through having anchored it at the end. The needle is then inserted on the other side and the procedure is repeated along the length of the wound resulting in one continuous stitch. The thread is then pulled taut and anchored at the other end. The survival suture kit consists of a curved surgical needle with attached thread. Is that any clearer?"

"Yep got that. Now you're going to tell me that these kits are readily available on-line."

"Right, and available from numerous suppliers too, so it really will be like searching for a needle in a haystack."

"Very droll Freddie but you were right to keep quiet about this, the press would have a field day and you can't trust the public to keep schtum. I presume he didn't do anything to the boy?"

"Nothing visible from the external exam but Jake, find the bastard quickly, this one's a nasty piece of work."

"Believe me, we'll try."

"I'll be doing the full PM on Monday, 'spect you'll want someone here."

The very thought made Jake feel squeamish but he said "yeah, probably me and DI Connolly."

"Heard she threw up when she discovered the bodies."

"Yeah, bloody bluebottles were the last straw. She's not easily sickened our Mo, usually known for having a cast iron stomach. Okay thanks Freddie, we'll be seeing you."

"Monday 10:30, date?"

"You got it."

16

The first thing Jake did when he arrived back at the station was photocopy the client list that Cora Allen had supplied. He glanced down the list and noticed that by the side of each name was a brief description. 'Very thorough Cora' he thought, as an image of the elegant woman popped into his head. There were eleven names in all, those that Cora obviously classed as Zoe's regulars.

He put the original list on his desk and then went in search of John Jackson. Jacko wasn't at his desk. Jake checked his watch and was surprised to see it was 13:15 already and that could only mean one thing, Jacko was in the staff canteen. Jake smiled, you could set a clock by Jacko's eating and drinking habits. He went back to his office and waited, and while he waited he examined the list in detail. The names were even in alphabetical order, doubtless the result of a tidy mind. Jake couldn't help himself, he had to add comments as he went through the list.

Men who always ask for Zoe if she's available:

X Arkin Alan - mid 40s, 5'11", short dark hair, dark brown eyes, scar under left eye, slightly overweight.

Jake put an X next to the name, Alan Arkin indeed Catch 22 American Movie Actor springs to mind

✓ Anderson Philip - 35+, 5'7", balding, bearded (ginger), wiry, nervous and tongue-tied.

Name could be legit

X Daniels Jack - 60+, 5'9", grey buzz cut, blue eyes, well-muscled body, exudes confidence, unable to fathom why he comes here!!!

Charcoal mellowed just like the whisky. I don't think so

✓ Finlay McDonald - early 30s, 6'2", name sounds Scottish but has no pronounced accent. Shoulder length mousey hair, hazel eyes, lanky frame, I expect his mother loves him.

Jake laughed out loud and ticked the name.

✓Garside Anthony - early 20s, 6', styled blonde hair, short at the sides, left long on top, green eyes, looks younger than he is. No job, no prospects, always arrogant, rich father Roland Garside entrepreneur.

Name is definitely genuine. He doesn't give a damn if other people know he comes to the club.

✓Hubbard Frank - late 40s early 50s, 6'6", shaved head, intense blue eyes, tattooed arms, toned body, scary to look at but according to Zoe kind, caring and considerate, a gentle giant.

Gentle giant or psychopath?

? Kunal Nikhil - about 40, 5' 5", dark haired, dark eyed, probably of Indian origin. Pencil moustache and goatee beard. Immaculate dresser, smells heavenly, wears lots of gold jewellery including a wedding band.

Who knows?

X Lawford Peter - mid 60s, 5'10", iron grey hair, short back and sides, blue/grey eyes, chiselled good looks, slim build. Casual dresser but only designer labels, usually wears Ray Bans, wealthy with a capital W.

Peter Lawford eh! TVs The Thin Man Nick Charles

✓Mitchell David - late 30s, 5'10", thinning sandy hair, pale blue eyes, Mr Average, insignificant. Not a snappy dresser but must have money, spends a lot of time at the Blue Lagoon.

Wimpy

X Matthews Bernard - early 40s, 5'10", short dark brown hair, blue eyes, wears heavy rimmed glasses, slim build, local accent. Non-descript sort of fellow, wouldn't think he's riveting company.

Talk Turkey

✓*Moran Richard - mid 40s, 6', shaggy brown hair with blonde highlights, blue eyes, lazy left eye, grossly overweight, always looks scruffy - his body just not made to hang clothes on. Unemployed, lives on money inherited from his aunt (or so he tells us constantly).*

Sounds delightful

Reading the descriptions made Jake smile, Cora Allen was obviously blessed with a sense of humour. She was obviously a good employer and protecting her girls seemed high on the agenda. In fact so diligent he almost expected to see snapshots beside each of the names. Of course, it was just a list, unfortunately not a list of suspects. But maybe, just maybe, the killer was lurking amongst them.

He heard the squad room door open and looking up saw Jacko ambling back in.

"Jacko, a minute please," he shouted through his open door.

"Guv?"

"I've got a job for you."

"Hallelujah, does that mean I can forget about Reggie Prentiss?"

"For now anyway, do you know The Blue Lagoon Club?"

"Yeah, high class knocking shop on Fenton Street."

"That's it, well one of the girls, Zoe Dryden, was found murdered at her home on Birchfield Avenue this morning and whoever was responsible killed her kid too. Freddie Saunders estimates time of death 72- to 84-hours ago. Cora Allen, who owns the club, has given us a list of Zoe's regular clients. What I need you to do is check out the names, find out which are genuine, if any, and an address would be good so we can get someone round to question them. Both Cora

Allen and Nick Danvers, the bar manager, have DI Connolly's mobile number and have promised to ring in if any of them turn up at the club. It will be late so the DI and me will cover it and take on-duty uniform with us if necessary."

Jake handed him the list.

"You'll see I've marked the names most likely to be real and scribbled a few flippant comments, just doodling really. But Jacko, check them all, maybe we really do have a local Alan Arkin."

"I'm on it Guv," Jacko said, turning to leave.

"Before you go, we need to locate Zoe Dryden's next of kin. Her sister appears to be it. She lives locally but's away in Cornwall on holiday with her family. We have Christian names Diana and Rob but no Surname, we don't know where in Cornwall they're staying but they live on Holderness Road on the North side of town. Cora Allen seems to think the husband is some sort of engineer who works locally. See if you can locate them."

"Anything else Guv?" Jacko asked, edging towards the door.

Jake, seeing he was literally chomping at the bit, dismissed him with "that's all for now thanks."

Jake smiled as Jacko scurried away given, a new purpose. The man was a force to be reckoned with.

17

Thirty minutes ago the squad room had resembled the Marie Celeste, lifeless and empty now it was buzzing with activity. Jake could hear the animated voices of Miller and Halliday, doubtless congratulating themselves on nabbing Hewitt. Mo was back from the Blue Lagoon, he could hear her moving about next door and Gregg and Grey had just arrived back from Birchfield Avenue. Everyone here, time to put them in the picture. Murder was the one crime that deserved a team effort. Jacko was already on the case, hopefully tracking down potential suspects.

The upstairs of the Station had undergone major refurbishment about three months ago, not a moment too soon in Jake's view. Fortunately, he was consulted before work began and was annoyed to find that newly promoted DI Connolly was to be given an office in the squad room and he would be stuck in one further along the top corridor. Privilege of rank, according to the powers that be. Privilege of rank be damned, he wouldn't be shoved into solitary confinement away from the cut and thrust of criminal investigation. So the powers that be capitulated, increased the size of the squad room and incorporated not one, but two offices. Leading off the squad room was a slightly smaller room nicknamed the 'boardroom' because it housed an executive- style oblong table seating 12 and capability for seating an additional 10-12 around the perimeter of the room. Large windows covered the left side wall making the room light and airy. Vertical blinds had been fitted to blot out the light for video and PC presentations. Two large whiteboards had been fixed to the right side wall. The room was ideal for squad meetings and as a major incident room.

Beyond CID was a large open plan office that housed the human resources team, civilians responsible for Recruitment, Personnel, and Training etc. Mike Long and his forensic team occupied the remainder of the upper floor. The laboratory and offices there were staffed by civilians and serving police officers, Mike being the SOCO in charge.

Mo tapped on Jake's door.

"Team's all here now Guv, shall we play catch up next door?"

"Great minds think alike. How do you feel about Barry Leyland sitting in? We may need Uniform's input at some point."

Mo straightened up, stepped back, clicked her heels and twiddled an imaginary moustache.

"Good call Sir."

Trying hard not to laugh at her irreverent impression of the stuffy, old fashioned copper Leyland, Jake said "assemble the troops next door and leave Inspector Leyland to me."

"Consider it done Guv, sorry, consider it done Sir," she replied, smiling smugly.

Unable to keep a straight face any longer, Jake just waved a dismissive hand.

"Get outta here Connolly."

"I'm going, I'm going."

Jake walked into the 'boardroom' followed, at a respective distance of course, by the ruddy faced Leyland. Jake's team were seated round the table chatting, and Mo was listening to Halliday excitedly telling her about his first collar as a DC.

"You know everyone Barry?"

"Yes Sir, I met your newest recruit for the first time yesterday."

Rhona Grey acknowledged the fact with a nod of her head.

"Okay have a seat. Inspector Connolly can tell us about Zoe Dryden."

Mo spent the next ten minutes describing the events that led to the discovery of the bodies and a further ten explaining what had happened since.

"So that's what we have to date, unless Dave and Rhona have gleaned anything from the neighbours. Dave?"

"Pretty pointless exercise really, most of the houses were empty. The people showing so much interest earlier must have left for work and those we did manage to question hadn't seen a thing. Guess the timing was wrong; it was after dark, they were probably all settled in front of Auntie Nelly." Realising the error of his ways, Gregg glanced over at Mo and saw her wince.

"Sorry Guv, in front of the telly."

It was Leyland's turn to grimace; the overfamiliar Guv used by CID obviously rankled him and it showed.

"Okay, thanks Dave. So what we've got is two murder victims, a list of Zoe Dryden's regulars that Jacko's working on and little else.

"Guv," Jacko interrupted, "I do have some information. I've already checked the one name that both you and Cora Allen thought was genuine. Anthony Garside is kosher. His father Roland is a well-known local business man, imports and distributes foods, beverages and wines from South America. Number 22 on Berkshire's rich list, he lives just up the road in Speen, place called Samdis Lodge. Naff name eh? Been morphed from South American and distribution, no doubt. There's a trophy wife in her late 20s and three sons from a previous marriage. Anthony is the youngest and by all accounts the black sheep. He describes himself as gainfully unemployed, whatever that means. In reality he's just a parasite living off his daddy's misplaced generosity. He's been pulled in several times for drunk driving, possession of cannabis, assault, you name it. Guess what? Roland bails him out."

"I get the distinct feeling this guy, and indeed the whole family, irritate you Jacko?"

"Yeah, I guess you're right. I can't stand people who think they're above the law just because they're rich."

"Point taken. So guys, where do we go from here?" Jake asked, waiting expectantly for an answer.

"Someone should talk to Garside as soon as possible, find out where he was on Monday night," Mo said.

We should get men back in Birchfield Avenue as soon people get home from work," Alan Miller added.

Gregg groaned in response to that idea.

"Hear that groan everyone? DC Gregg has just volunteered to take the overtime for Birchfield. Any more takers?" Jake asked.

Halliday spluttered attempting to suppress a laugh and failing miserably.

"Good, Halliday seems to think it'll be fun too so you can take him along with you," Jake said, looking directly at Dave Gregg.

"I can let you have Evans if you need any help with that," Leyland offered.

"Thanks Barry, but I'm sure Gregg and Halliday can manage."

"Jacko, does Anthony Garside live at the family home in Speen?"

"That's the address he's always given when he's been nicked."

"Okay, Alan get over there now."

Mo, noticing disappointment on the face of CID's newest recruit, added "and Alan take DC Grey with you."

"That was kind," Jake murmured, when everyone else had left the 'boardroom.'

"Jake, get real, I don't do kind. I just thought she's a good cop, she should spend time out there doing what good cops do best. She was working on the Jamieson case but Gregg and Halliday seem keen to question potential witnesses, so I'll hand it over to them for now. Good practise eh?"

"You're all heart Connolly."

"You've been talking to Jess again," she quipped, green eyes twinkling with mischief.

"You're incorrigible."

"And aren't you the lucky one, having me as a colleague and friend."

Banter over it was time to get serious.

"We've got a child killer out there Mo and I want him caught quickly so, if you agree, I'd like to involve the whole team in this inquiry. Not to the detriment of ongoing investigations, of course, but solving a murder rates high on our list of priorities."

"I agree, they're a good bunch and each has different strengths, let's use them. Talking of strengths, I'll hand over the Jamieson inquiry to Happy and Grumpy. That should keep the pair of them busy until they're on door knocking duty tonight."

She went over to Rhona's desk, flicked open the file, spent several minutes reading the notes and then walked purposefully towards Dave Gregg.

Before Jake had time to close his office door Jacko was following him in.

"Diana and Robert Preston married 2003, two sons Marshall 10 and Robert junior 8."

The puzzled look on Jake's face made Jacko realise he hadn't quite grasped the significance of what he was hearing.

"Sorry Guv, Zoe Dryden's sister, Diana, married a Robert Preston in 2003."

"You know this how?"

"On line birth, marriage and death records. I assumed Diana's maiden name was Dryden and the rest was easy. He's a design engineer with Digby Mechanical and Industrial Engineering in Thatcham. Information courtesy of 'LinkedIn', the on-line professional network. Oh and Zoe's parents are Duncan and Mary Preston, they lived in Derbyshire when the girls were born. Where they are now is anybody's guess."

"I'm impressed Jacko, it's taken you all of ten minutes to come up with that important info."

"Thanks Guv, but it's remarkably easy. All the information's out there, you just have to know how to access it."

"Just keep on accessing it, that's all I ask."

Jake went next door and found Mo hunched over her lap top, one hand unconsciously raking through her spiky blonde hair and so completely absorbed in something that she was oblivious to his presence.

"Mo."

"Christ Jake, you made me jump, I was miles away."

"I can tell, what's on your mind?"

"Just something Cora said."

"And?"

"She said Zoe didn't see clients at home. So doesn't it follow that the murderer is unlikely to be a John, regular or otherwise?"

"Maybe he was obsessed, found out where she lived and visited anyway."

"But then why would she let him into the house?"

"Perhaps she didn't have a choice. I agree it does seem unlikely, but we have to start somewhere. We've been given a list of names, some I'm sure are the result of a good imagination but let's find out who they are and check 'em out anyway."

"Yeah, yeah, I wasn't suggesting otherwise, just mulling things over in my mind and you did ask."

"Serves me right then, and Mo, never stop mulling things over, that's what makes you the second smartest officer in the squad."

"The first being?" she laughed.

"Modesty forbids me to answer that."

Mo laughed again "you don't know the meaning of modesty!"

"Joking aside, I came to tell you that Jacko has found out that Rob Preston, Zoe's brother-in-law, works at Digby Engineering in Thatcham. Wanna take a ride out there?"

"Indeedy"

"Okay grab your coat and let's go."

18

Digby Engineering was housed in the industrial heartland of Thatcham. Glass walls spanned two sides of the three story flat roofed building which nestled serenely in landscaped gardens, making the numerous industrial units on either side look positively shabby.

"Wow, didn't expect to see a modern building like this in the middle of an industrial estate. Who owns it?" Mo asked, as they walked towards reception from the Visitors Car Park.

"No idea, but we're about to find out," Jake said, pushing open the glass doors that led to reception.

Inside the building plush red carpet stretched wall to wall. In stark contrast the semi-circular reception desk to the right was black with a light wood trim. Two girls sat behind it, a redhead was bent over a computer keyboard the other, a brown eyed brunette, smiled and said "welcome to Digby Engineering, how may we help?"

Jake showed his warrant card.

"DCI Summers and DI Connolly, we believe a Robert Preston is an employee here". The brunette nodded and the redhead looked up open-mouthed, neither said a word.

"I take that as a yes, he does work here."

The brunette nodded again.

"We need to contact him as a matter of urgency," Jake said, fixing the mute pair with a quizzical look.

Finally coming out of her trance the brunette said "he's not here."

"We know, we need to talk to someone who might know where he is?"

"HR will know," the redhead said, looking extremely pleased with herself. "It's company policy to leave a contact address with them."

"Well, can we speak to someone in HR?"

"I'll ring and ask if someone will see you."

Mo could sense the waves of impatience radiating from Jake's tense body so before he could get really angry she interrupted.

"You haven't quite grasped this have you lady? We're the police, we're here and we need to speak to someone regarding Rob Preston, now."

The redhead, giving Mo a drop dead look, did as she was told.

After a brief conversation on the phone the redhead, identified by her badge as Paula, said "take a seat someone will be down shortly."

"Thanks, I was just about to hit meltdown," Jake said, as they sat down in the leather armchairs located to the left of the entrance and just in front of the lift doors.

"I know, faced with dumb and dumber who wouldn't?" she whispered wickedly.

Moments later the lift doors opened revealing a short, skinny middle aged man with grey hair. Mo fully expected him to say "I'm free" cos he was the spit of Mr Humphries from 'Are you being served.'

Instead, he extended an outstretched hand to Jake and said in a rich baritone voice "Michael Edwards, Head of Human Resources."

Jake shook his hand.

"DCI Summers, my colleague DI Connolly."

Mo shook his hand. She wanted to giggle, the man had a grip of iron, nothing like the limp handed Humphries.

"So officers, what's our Rob been up to?"

"What makes you think he's been up to anything?"

"Paula told me you wanted to talk about Rob Preston so I assumed he'd done something to warrant your interest."

Let me put your mind at rest on that score Mr Edwards, Rob Preston has done nothing to warrant our interest but we do need to contact him. Your receptionist Paula said you would know how."

"He's on holiday in Cornwall."

"We know that much, do you have a contact address?"

Edwards reluctantly fished out a sheet of paper from his top pocket and handed it to Jake.

"Hotel Miramar, Portland Road, St Ives."

"Thanks for your help," Jake said, taking the address from him and turning to leave.

"Is that it?"

"That's it," Jake said.

"Aren't you going tell me what this is all about?"

"I'm afraid not Sir, we can't discuss police business with the public."

"But the man works here."

"Then ask him, it's his decision then whether or not he chooses to tell you."

Edwards showed his irritation to Jake's answer with a petulant shake of his head and a dismissive "well if that's all, I'll get back to work." Without another word he turned his back on them and walked towards the lift.

"Thank again," Jake shouted after him but he didn't even have the courtesy to face them, just lifted his arm in acknowledgement.

Jake looked at Mo raised his eyebrows.

"I think we're done here."

Jake could tell she was bursting to say something and as soon as they were outside she did.

"Used to getting his own way, pompous little prick. Impressive put down though."

"Well he got nothing and we got what we came for, I'd call that a result wouldn't you?"

"Result," she said, raising her hand for a high five.

Driving back to the station Mo volunteered to liaise with the local police in St Ives and ask them to deliver the news to the Preston family. A traumatic job at the best of times but it needed to be done in person, not over the phone.

"Oh and I have a snippet from Freddie Saunders. Our killer, seriously weird, stitched up Zoe Dryden's vagina."

"What?" Mo said, turning her head to look at him in disbelief.

"He stitched up Zoe's vagina, what'd make of that?"

"That's something you need to discuss with Jaime, she's the psychologist. But if you're asking my opinion then the fucker's a control freak."

"Exactly my thoughts but I will talk to Jaime. What's the point of having a trained psychologist in the family and not making use of her? She's on our side."

"I bloody hope so, she'd be a dangerous adversary."

Jake laughed. "One I can wrap round my little finger."

"If you believe that you live in cloud cuckoo land Mr."

19

When they walked back into the squad room Jacko looked up from his computer.

"Gregg and Halliday have gone to interview the Nickerson woman. Oh and I've managed to sort out which of the Johns are genuine. Shall I bring the list in?"

"That'd be good."

"I'll join you in a minute Guv; I need to get in touch with St Ives first."

"Give us five then Jacko, not much point in going over the info twice."

Fifteen minutes later the three of them were in Jake's office crowded round Jacko's amended list.

"I've listed the ones I think are genuine names first. Garside you already know about but six of the other names look pretty kosher too, including Jack Daniels and Bernard Matthews. I'm concentrating on those we can identify so they can be interviewed, the others will be trickier. It's knowing where to start."

"I have every faith in you."

"It may well be misplaced we'll see."

"You've done remarkably well so far. So how much do we know about these guys?"

"Well I've tracked down info on three. Jack Daniels, a retired business man, lived in Granada in Spain for years. He owned several hotels throughout Andalusia, including five star establishments in Granada itself, Malaga and Cordoba. His wife Nicole died five years ago so he sold up and came back to the UK. Lives just up the road from here in Cold Ash, close to his married daughter.

Finlay McDonald lives with his parents, they're arable farmers in Boxford."

"Where's Boxford?" Jake asked.

"Picturesque village 4-miles north west of here, sits on the east bank of the river Lambourn. Nice place, nice pub, you should go." Mo replied.

"Never heard of it."

"I'm not surprised, you're hardly a local lad are you Guv?" Jake ignored the jibe.

"Sorry Jacko, you were saying McDonald lives there."

"Not much else to say about him Guv, he's unmarried, works and lives on the family farm.

Then we get to Nikhil Kunal, his parents Canda and Lira were expelled from Uganda in 1972. They settled in Newbury in '75. Canda, despite his unfortunate circumstances, was determined to succeed and over the next twenty years built up a successful pharmaceutical company. Nikhil, their second son, was born in London in 1973 making him 41. He's married, has three children and lives in Newbury. He claims to be stuck in an arranged marriage, likes the ladies and is known to favour European women.

That's all I have for you at the moment. I'm still working on the others."

"Brilliant Jacko, thank you."

"Do you want Daniels or McDonald?" Jake asked Mo.

"Given a choice, I'll take Daniels."

"Then you've got him. I'll go see the farm boy. We'll meet back here later and compare notes. We may even get time to see Kunal." Jake looked at his watch, it was 2:24 pm. "Let's aim to be back here by 4:30 pm so we can have a de-brief in the 'boardroom'."

Twenty minutes later Mo pulled into the driveway of Sawden House, Cold Ash Hill. It didn't live up to expectations. She assumed, wrongly it seemed, that the wealthy Daniels would live in some sort of mansion. Instead she was parked in front of a fairly modest detached house, in its own grounds granted, but far from grandiose. Her footsteps crunched on the gravel drive as she walked to the front door. She rang the bell, moments later the door was answered by a handsome grey-haired man looking much like the description Cora had given. Like Cora, she didn't understand his need for the company of prostitutes.

"Mr Jack Daniels?"

"That's me."

"DI Connolly, Thames Valley Police," Mo said, showing her warrant card.

"DI eh? Can't be about speeding then. How can I help?"

"Perhaps we can talk inside Sir."

"Sorry, yes come on in."

He led the way through the hall into a comfortable sitting room where he offered her a seat.

He sat down opposite and asked again "so DI Connolly, how can I help?"

"I believe you know Zoe Dryden."

"Do I?" He asked, looking puzzled.

"You may know her as Candice, she works at the Blue Lagoon Club in Newbury."

"Yeah I know Candice, lovely girl."

"Are you a client?"

"How is that any of your business Inspector?"

"It became my business when she was found murdered earlier today, Sir"

"Oh my God, she can't be dead," Daniels said, burying his head in his hands.

When he looked up again Mo noticed tears in his eyes so unless the man was a good actor he was genuinely upset.

"She was killed today you say?"

"No she was found today. When did you last see Zoe, Mr Daniels?"

"About ten days ago at the club. Why? You can't seriously think I had anything to do with her death. It wasn't just the sex you know, I was lonely, we talked and she listened. She was a friend."

"I'm not accusing you of anything but we do need to eliminate you from our enquiries. So can I ask where you were on Monday and Tuesday of this week?"

"That's easy, I've been staying at my daughter's house since last Saturday. She's been in hospital giving birth to her third child. I've been there looking after the house and babysitting the kids while her husband visited. She's coming home today so I came back here about 10am this morning, after the kids went off to school."

"We will have to confirm your story."

"Be my guest, I've got nothing to hide. Just promise me you'll catch the bastard who killed Zoe."

"We'll do our best." Mo stood up ready to leave. Daniels stood too and shook her outstretched hand.

"Thanks for your time Mr Daniels and I'm sorry about being the bearer of bad news."

"Me too. Zoe was a lovely person, why would anyone kill her?"

"Because they could I guess. Thanks again and by the way, congratulations on your new grandchild."

Daniels smiled. Just a gesture of acknowledgement, Mo could tell his heart wasn't in it. He stood on the doorstep and watched her drive away.

She glanced at her watch it was still only 3:17pm, enough time to pay Nikhil Kunal a visit.

20

Jake meanwhile was eating a homemade scone in a farmhouse kitchen under the watchful eye of Fiona McDonald, a large buxom woman whom he judged to be in her mid-sixties. The heat in the kitchen was stifling, feeling beads of sweat forming on his brow he wiped them away with the heel of his hand and loosened his tie.

"Warm in here?" he said, looking up at her.

"Aye, 'at will be t' bakin'," she replied in a hard to understand Glaswegian accent. Although her ruddy complexion was getting redder by the minute, she seemed oblivious to the heat but the twinkle in her blue eyes made him think she was enjoying his discomfort.

According to his mother Finlay wasnae at haim, he was fence mendin' on th' Forty Acre Field. She'd rung his mobile, told him to gie himself haem and then insisted Jake had tea and freshly baked scones whilst waiting.

"Finlay doesnae hae mony social graces but he's a good loon, works stoaner tay."

Unable to fully understand her, Jake could tell she was worried by his refusal to tell her the nature of his business with her son and could only assume she was trying to extol his virtues.

The back door flung open providing a blast of cool air, for which Jake was more than grateful. A man in his thirties stood in the entrance unlacing black work boots which he left on the doorstep before stepping inside. Homely looking was being generous; lank mousey hair hung to his shoulders framing a thin pointed face, his hazel eyes were heavy lidded and set too close together and poor posture made him look shorter than his 6'5". Even Cora had misjudged the man's height by a good three inches.

Jake stood, held out his hand and introduced himself. Finlay ignored the outstretched hand, his eyes darting around the room nervously and totally avoiding any eye contact.

"Finlay!" his mother shouted, making Jake jump. Finlay suddenly snapped to attention and looked first at his mother and then at Jake.

"He suffers frae attention deficit disorder amongst other things," she explained, shrugging her shoulders.

"I'm afraid that's true," a voice said from outside. Jake looked towards the door and saw a well-muscled man in his later thirties standing in the entrance to the kitchen. He was shorter than Finlay, around six foot, was dressed in jeans and a plaid shirt and was holding Jake's gaze with steely blue eyes.

"I'm Iain McDonald, Fin's brother. How can we help you Inspector?"

'No trace of a Scottish accent thank God' Jake thought, and realising it must have been Iain not Finlay that Fiona McDonald had phoned simply said "I need to know Finlay's whereabouts on Monday and Tuesday of this week."

"That's easy, he was here. He's always here."

"Not strictly true is it Mr McDonald? We know for a fact he visits the Blue Lagoon club in Newbury and, furthermore, he's a regular client of Zoe Dryden who works there."

"Ye tauld me 'er nam was Candice," Fiona McDonald blurted out.

"She calls herself Candice, her real name could be Greta Garbo for all I care. A mate recommended her, said she would take good care of Fin. I take Fin to the club once a month on a Friday, he may have his problems but he's a man for God's sake. He still has urges like the rest of us so I take him, wait for him in the bar, and bring him home afterwards. Why do you need to know his whereabouts anyway?"

"Because Zoe Dryden was found murdered at her home in Birchfield Avenue."

"And you suspect Fin? You're having a laugh. The poor sod couldn't even find his way home if I wasn't around. "

Finlay McDonald still hadn't spoken, just looked trustingly at his older brother.

"Finlay wooldnae hurt a fly."

"I'm sure he wouldn't Mrs McDonald, but surely you realise we have to check on everyone who knew Zoe."

"So you've checked, now you can leave."

"Dornt be rude Iain he's only daein' his job."

"Well maybe, but his job's done here."

Jake, deciding Iain McDonald was probably right, stood up, shook hands with Fiona McDonald and left convinced that Finlay probably didn't even know the time of day. It was 4.04pm, just time to get back to the station.

21

At 4:25pm Jake walked into an empty squad room. Hearing voices, he walked towards the 'boardroom' and stuck his head round the door. Most of the team were already gathered there. The one notable absentee was Mo.

"Guv," Miller said, spotting him. With that one word chit chat ceased, backs straightened in seats and heads tuned towards the door.

"DI Connolly not back yet?"

A sharp tap on his left shoulder made him spin round.

"She is now," Mo said, smiling.

"What kept you?"

She glanced at her watch and tapped it.

"4:27pm, Tag Heuer accuracy tells me I made it with time to spare."

"It tells me that DIs are paid far too much if they can afford Tag Heuer watches," he whispered.

They joined the others round the table.

"Okay, now everyone's here we can make a start. Let's deal with the Jamieson inquiry first. Dave, Steve, anything to report?"

"Quite a lot actually Guv. Joanna Nickerson was adamant that Christine Jamieson's death was no accident. She also apologised profusely about keeping quiet until now. We took her statement, it was much the same as she'd already told uniform. We checked the partial number plate ID against vehicles reported stolen and got lucky. A silver Vauxhall saloon registration RK61 AFC was taken from a local factory car park two weeks ago. Owner, a Brad Pearson, reported it missing when he finished work for the day and wanted to drive home. He was pretty miffed too; the car apparently was his pride and joy, the first brand new one he'd ever been able to afford, gone. There were no sightings of the vehicle prior to the incident and have been none since. The husband, Paul Jamieson, was at work at the time the incident took place and verified by his secretary Deirdre Phillips, so we can probably rule him out as a suspect. That's it so far, obviously we need to find out more about the victim, enemies, affairs anything that could lead to her being a target for some murderous Bob Dylan."

"Villain Guv, he means murderous villain," Steve Halliday painstakingly explained when Jake looked exasperated.

"Okay good progress there, keep digging. Right, let's get to Zoe Dryden. Alan, tell us about Anthony Garside"

"The bloke's an absolute arse but he didn't kill Zoe or Zak, that's for sure. He's been in hospital for the past 6-days, involved in some sort of fracas in Bristol. Apparently tried to chat some girl up in a pub there, didn't take no for an answer and was given a pretty severe beating by the boyfriend and several of the boyfriend's mates. He's currently languishing in a private room in the Bristol Royal Infirmary courtesy of dad Roland's private healthcare scheme. His step mother, Danielle ..."

"Call me Dannie," Rhona interrupted, giving a girlish giggle and making everyone smile.

Despite being interrupted even Miller smiled before continuing, "... yes, thank you Rhona, as I was saying, Danielle seemed to delight in telling us that Garside was suffering from multiple contusions, two broken ribs, a broken wrist, a fractured tibia and concussion, amongst other things. So he's definitely out of the frame for this one."

"Thanks Alan, that brings us to our Tennessee Whisky man Jack Daniels."

"No go there either, I'm afraid. He hadn't seen Zoe for 10-days, spent almost all of the last week living at his daughter's house looking after his grandchildren while she was giving birth to her third child. His alibi is sound and he seemed genuinely upset when he heard that Zoe was dead. She wasn't just a prostitute to him, she was a friend with benefits. I liked the man."

"Inspector Connolly likes the man and I trust her instincts, so that brings us to Finlay McDonald."

"Not quite Guv, I had time to pay Nikhil Kunal a visit too."

"Did you like him?"

"No."

"Looks like we have our first suspect," Jake joked, initiating a round of applause.

"Sorry Mo, just trying to lighten the mood a little. Tell us about Mr Kunal."

"Seriously rich, he's MD of the family pharmaceutical company. He's arrogant, self-obsessed and utterly repugnant. And that's just for starters. He takes business associates to the Blue Lagoon on a regular basis and that's how he first met Zoe who, by the way, meant nothing to him. Quote 'she was a good looking whore who opened her legs for money' unquote. He wouldn't dream of associating with her in the real world. Apparently he has more than enough so called respectable women to cater for his gargantuan sexual appetite, his words not mine. Obnoxious little weasel Guv, but I don't think he's a killer. He doesn't have a motive, besides he's small and slight and I don't honestly think he has the strength to kill anyone."

"Alibi?"

"Daisy Coombs, or was it Helena Bainbridge, one or the other or maybe both, he couldn't remember. But we should ask them, after all he, apparently, is far more memorable than they are. As I said before, an arrogant piece of shit."

"Well Finlay McDonald isn't our man either. He has a low IQ, probably suffers from some sort of Asperger's syndrome and doesn't leave the house unless accompanied by his brother. The brother, Iain, takes him to the club once a month, pays for him to have sex and then escorts him home again. Apparently Zoe was recommended for her caring nature, nothing more. So that's four down seven to go. Any progress on the others Jacko?"

"Some Guv. Frank Hubbard, 48, divorced local builder, owns Hubbard Construction based in Thatcham. My mate Harvey's brother works for him, says he's a good bloke to work for, pays well and treats his employees fairly. They're building a small development of luxury homes on the south side of Newbury. Hubbard is a hands-on sort of guy, turns up on site on a daily basis and works alongside his men. So he's easy to find Monday through Saturday.

Richard Moran, unemployed, doesn't claim benefits, doesn't need to. Aunt, Clara Meyers, left him just over £25million fifteen years ago. She was his mother's sister, widow of Carl Meyers the retail magnate. No kids of her own, Moran probably wormed his way into her affections and bingo, at 30 he's a multi-millionaire. The remainder of the Meyer's fortune went to charity.

He owns a big house on Bloomfield Road, employs a cook, gardener and housekeeper. Likes a flutter on the horses and loves spending time at the Racecourse. No significant other, visits the Blue Lagoon on a regular basis.

Philip Anderson, 36, academic, Professor of Archaeology and Ancient History at the University of Reading. This guy lives alone in a cottage in Aldermaston, a village halfway between Newbury and Reading.

The others are proving more difficult, Alan Arkin, Peter Lawford, David Mitchell and Bernard Matthews. I can't find anything on these guys, they've probably given false names and we may well have to wait for 'em to go back to the club before we can track 'em down."

"Yeah, I was never hopeful about Arkin, Lawford and Matthews but Mitchell, well he could've been kosher. Nonetheless you've done well Jacko. We need to talk to the guys you've identified and keep our fingers crossed about the rest."

"David Mitchell is quite a common name and there are several in the area but none match the description we've been given, and most of them couldn't afford a drink at the Blue Lagoon never mind the price of a high class 'tom'."

Jake looked up at the wall clock it was 5.24pm.

"I think we can call it a day. Dave, Steve take a break before you go back to Birchfield Avenue and fellas, thanks for volunteering. Tomorrow's another day, we'll divvy out the list then and pay a few more visits so enjoy your evening and goodnight."

"Well thank you Guv," Gregg said, with more than a hint of sarcasm.

"You're welcome Dave, believe me you're very welcome."

Mo and Jake were the last to leave, the others scattered like leaves with a force ten behind them, anxious to avoid any last minute good ideas the bosses might have.

"They must all be on a Friday night promise," Jake said, laughing.

"Rhona's going home to her GP, Alan's got a hot date with a leggy blonde and Jacko, well Jacko's in love with his PC. Calls it Sally you know?"

"You know all of this, how?"

"They confide in me."

"Why?"

"Because deep down I'm still one of them and they know it."

"And I'm not?"

"No, you came here as the Guv and that's what you'll always be to them. But believe this, they like and respect you."

"I'll settle for that and rely on you to tell me their secrets."

"Only those I'm allowed to tell."

"Any plans this evening."

"Yeah we're out to dinner."

"Anywhere nice?"

"New place in Leckhampstead called 'Chez Summers'. The owner, a Jaime Summers, invited Jess and told her to bring a friend. I hear they do a very good pasta bake, now who could possibly refuse an offer like that?"

Jake laughed. "No one, see you later then."

"Pasta bake and a bottle of red, indeed you will."

22

"My compliments to the chef," Mo said, making herself comfortable beside Jess on one of the tan leather settees that flanked a large slate topped coffee table in the centre of the sitting room. They were all feeling relaxed and mellow after consuming a Jaime Summers speciality of a Penne Pasta Bake, served with Caesar salad and garlic Ciabatta, washed down with a bottle of Chianti. Jaime had made a delicious Tiramisu to follow. Completely stuffed, Mo and Jake weaved their tipsy way through into the sitting room. Following the surer pathway already made by the sobriety sisters, Jess and Jaime. Both had good reasons for remaining sober, Jess was driving and Jaime was pregnant. Jess smiled knowingly as Mo settled beside her. Someone would be complaining of a sore head in the morning.

"Brandy anyone?" Jake said, addressing everyone but looking directly at Mo.

"Better not, I've already sunk half a bottle of Chianti and we're working tomorrow remember?"

"Good point, Inspector Connolly, we've probably had enough then."

Jaime looked up at her husband smiled and said "sit down honey before you fall down. You're working tomorrow, splendid. That means you won't be here to moan when I go and see Kate Davis."

"You're seeing Kate tomorrow? I thought you'd finished delving into that past life regression thing." Jess said, her ears pricking up at the mention of a friend's name.

"I have, but she phoned and asked for a meeting. Apparently a client's given her a false name and address after a consultation so the tape and notes she sent to him were returned with address unknown. The address he gave, Patrick Street, was kosher until 7-years ago when the houses were demolished to make way for the new library. Apparently it was big news at the time, demonstrations and the like, people arrested."

"Yeah, I remember officers trying to keep the peace outside the council offices one day when demonstrators started pelting councillors with eggs. The planning officer had his car tyres slashed too. Seemed none of the residents wanted to be ousted from their homes on the whim of some bureaucrat on the town council and really who could blame them. Let's just say the police had a presence there but I don't think they stopped many eggs from reaching their targets," Mo said, conjuring up the picture of an egg spattered Jeremy Perkins on the front page of the local rag.

"Very professional, Leyland couldn't have been IC then otherwise he'd have hauled their sorry arses straight back to the nick," Jake said, smiling.

Jaime punched him lightly on the arm and said "Can I finish this story or what?"

"Be my guest darling."

"Well, the really fascinating thing about this story is the fact that a guy called James Mitchell used to live at the address given to Kate."

"Don't tell me that was the name he gave too?" It was Jess that interrupted this time.

"No, more bizarre than that. He gave the name David Mitchell who was James's son and who was killed back in 2001."

Jake looked at Mo and said "David Mitchell, we've found David Mitchell."

"What the hell are you talking about? The man's dead and Kate's understandably worried as to her client's reasons for giving a dead man's name and address."

All signs of intoxication vanished; Jake and Mo were suddenly alert and functioning police officers.

"One very good reason he doesn't want her to know his true identity and, coincidentally, we are also unable to trace a David Mitchell who could be involved in our current inquiry."

"Which is?" Jaime asked, intrigued as only a writer could be.

So Jake spent the next 20-minutes telling them.

"So do you think these two men could be one and the same?" Jess asked, looking at Mo.

"Well it's one hell of a coincidence if they're not. Two men calling themselves David Mitchell, one's dead and the other's untraceable, I'd lay money on it." Mo said excitedly.

"But before we get too excited we still don't know his true identity," Jaime said.

Jake, noticing the sudden use of we, laughed and said "so we're all working the case now."

"Who better to have on board than a crime writer who always gets her man. And not forgetting that said novelist is also a trained Clinical Psychologist with profiling skills."

"Well then no worries, we have it sewn up. I look forward to hearing what your friend Kate has to say about our Mr Mitchell."

"I'm coming with you tomorrow," Jess said, looking directly at Jaime.

She didn't argue and that's how their evening came to a close. Jess promising to pick Jaime up the following morning and Mo telling Jake she'd see him at the station bright and early.

23

Saturday and Mark Forrester sat on the bench outside the fitness centre on Park Road. He'd sat here every Saturday morning for the last month, hoping to catch a glimpse of the stunning woman that was Natalya Birinov. Five weeks ago, for his 21st birthday, his twin brothers, Owen and Luke, had booked a table at The Blue Lagoon. After the meal they'd organised a night of liquor and lust with three of the club hostesses. The boys saved for over a year to pay for this treat and, being 24-year-old young men with raging hormones, had decided to include themselves in the deal. As Luke so rightly said "Unus pro omnibus, omnes pro uno, translated for you dear brother one for all and all for one". That had made Mark laugh out loud because for as long as he could remember their dad, Aaron, had referred to them as the three musketeers. And that was the night he'd first seen the delightful Natalya. At a statuesque five foot nine she was almost as tall as him, her honey blonde hair hung in waves about her shoulders, her midnight blue eyes framed by thick lashes were her most outstanding feature and gazing into them Mark had been lost. It was certainly a night he would remember forever and meeting up with his brothers the following morning all he could talk about was Natalya.

After a conversation where every other sentence started Natalya said this Natalya did that, Owen looked at Luke raised his eyebrows.

"She must have been something really special, I think the young one's in lust or is it love Mark?"

Mark leaned over and punching his brother's arm answered a tad too quickly.

"Don't be daft, she's a pro not the girl next door."

"Methinks he doth protest too much," Luke said, stroking his chin theatrically.

"And methinks you're a pair of prats," Mark said, grinning.

But they'd been right, he was smitten and because Natalya happened to say she went to the Park Road Gym every Saturday at 9am he'd camped outside every Saturday since. On the first occasion she'd seen him, waved and came over to say hello. He'd asked her out to lunch. She replied in her husky accented voice.

"Sorry Mark, I don't date clients. Anyway, honestly you're far too young, you're certainly cute but you still have freckles," she said stroking the bridge of his nose.

"I'm 21," he said, looking upset.

"And I'm 27 going on 40," she said, turning and walking away.

Since then she'd just ignored his presence until today. Today, looking angry she came over and said "are you stalking me?"

"No, just hoping you'll change your mind about lunch. Will you?"

"Never, as I told you already you're too young and, believe this, you can't afford me."

Looking hurt and dejected he got up and walked away from her. Glancing back a moment later he saw her leaning into a red sports car laughing. She got in and they drove past him without even a glance. Jealous, he stared after the man that had captured her attention. He looked old, probably about 40 with thinning sandy hair. Suddenly he realised just how stupid he'd been, she obviously worshipped at the altar of wealth if she preferred an old man like that to a young good looking guy like him. Well there was always Georgie Adams, she'd made it pretty obvious she fancied him and Natalya, from being the love of his life became just another pricey whore.

24

Damn, she's lost to me, she's talking to some boy outside the gym. No, thank you God, she's sent him packing. I wind down the window and call her. She screws up her eyes and peers towards the car. Then she smiles, raises her hand in greeting, walks over and leans towards the open window.

"Sorry, can't remember your name but I know you from the club don't I?"

"Yeah. David's the name, David Mitchell."

"So David, what're you doing here?"

"Just happened to be passing, saw you and it got me thinking that maybe, just maybe, you'd like to earn a little extra cash."

"How little?"

"Say £500."

Without another word she's sliding into the passenger seat of the car, not my car but the one I borrowed from the car park outside Farradays. A red Merc Convertible parked in the bay marked Samuel F. Farraday , Company Director. It won't be missed before tonight, I know for a fact that dear old Sam's a workaholic and careless. He leaves a spare key to his Merc taped to the underside of the front wheel arch. I glance at the lovely Natalya Birinov; her high cheekbones, fine features, and honey blonde hair remind me of a young Michelle Pfeiffer. I have to remind myself that she's just another common whore, totally disloyal to her employer having agreed my price, as I knew she would.

"Where to?"

"I have a house on Dereham Street, you know it?"

"I know it."

"Good," she said, placing a well-manicured hand on my thigh, "then let's go."

I feel empowered by the adrenaline rush of anticipation. 'Home James and don't spare the horses' goes through my mind. I switch on the engine and pull sharply away from the kerb, making the tyres squeal in protest.

"Oh my we are impatient," she laughs, stroking my inner thigh.

Feeling the sudden bulge in my jeans I remove her hand and hiss "if I get to fuck you fine, you get your money, if I come in my pants deals off."

Startled by the malice in my voice she eases back into her seat.

"Okay, okay relax, just trying to be friendly."

"Sorry bad week," I explain, not wanting to scare her yet, that will come later.

"You seem different somehow."

"No just the same old mild mannered man I've always been."

I glance at her again, see her raise her eyebrows in disbelief, and start talking endless drivel hoping to persuade her I am good old harmless David. By the time we reach Dereham Street she's convinced.

The upwardly mobile thirty somethings have chosen Dereham Street, with its tree lined pavements and eclectic mix of detached and semi-detached houses, as their own. I doubt they realise a prostitute is living amongst them. They'll find out soon enough. The thought makes me smile.

"Over there on the left, number 26," she says, pointing towards a modest detached house with a red front door.

'How fitting' I think, pulling up in front of it. It's detached, that's a real bonus, no noise worries. I look at my watch it's 11.45am.

Before getting out I cover my head with the navy hoodie I'm wearing and then follow her to the door. I don't want any nosey neighbours giving my description to the cops. I've never wear jeans and a hoodie, not my style so I'll just dump them later. The cars not mine so I figure I have my arse covered.

Well we're finally here, now the fun really begins.

She walks to the door looks at me and grins, "no need to hide behind the hoodie, no one in the neighbourhood knows I'm a hooker, they think I'm into interior design. That is everyone except Brad Schofield at number 42. He's a frequent visitor to the club but he certainly wouldn't want anyone to find out, especially the wealthy father-in-law who employs him.

She opens the door still smiling.

"Come in David."

I follow her inside, the bulge in my pants is back with a vengeance.

25

The morning had been a frustrating one for Mo and Jake. Gregg and Halliday had nothing to report. Residents of Birchfield Avenue had neither seen nor heard anything that would be of the slightest help to their inquiry. Dave Gregg said it was as if everyone shut their front doors after work and locked out the rest of the world 'til the following morning.

Jacko came in to beaver over his computer but the remaining four guys still remained untraceable. Explaining what happened last night, Jake asked him to concentrate on Mitchell. He quickly found the information about the dead guy on line but no indication about who the man calling himself Mitchell was. Jacko explored all the possibilities he could think of. If the guy knew Mitchell's name, knew where he lived and knew he was dead then surely it followed that he knew Mitchell personally. So maybe he was a friend, a family member or even a work colleague. Zilch. So Jacko was feeling frustrated too. How the hell were they going to find this guy and when, or if, they did would he be the man they were actually looking for.

Having been on duty last night, Gregg and Halliday were more than pleased to be sent home until Monday. Jake went to see Moran, Mo went for the academic, leaving DS Miller and DC Grey to don hard hats and visit a building site.

Moran didn't disappoint, he was exactly what Jake was expecting. He had the Triple F Factor, Flaccid Fat and Forties. He was reluctant to let Jake into the house.

"There's a meeting on at the Racecourse, first race is 1:30 pm and if we don't get going soon we'll be late for pre-race hospitality."

"Then if necessary you'll miss it Sir. I'm here investigating a woman's death, a woman, I'm told, that you knew intimately. What's more important, the death of someone you knew or a dish of strawberries and cream?"

Moran actually had the good grace to blush as he finally opened the door enough for Jake to enter.

"Sorry forgetting my manners, come in."

"Who is it Ricky?" a girlie voice said from behind the mountainous Moran.

"Nothing to worry you sugar? Just need a minute to speak to the policeman and then we'll be off," he said, turning towards a busty, frizzy haired, blonde who looked young enough to be his daughter.

"Ooh a policeman and a tall dark handsome one at that, what'ya bin doing Ricky?"

"Nothing sugar, they want to rope me in on some charity do, you go chose a bauble from the catalogue, it won't take long."

At the mention of a bauble she scuttled away and Moran led Jake into what looked like a home office and closed the door behind them.

"So what's this about?"

They quickly established that Moran had been one of Zoe's regulars, although he hadn't been near the club for at least three months and had a cast iron alibi in the shape of the blonde bimbo.

"You met my fiancée Tammy, isn't she something? We got together 15-weeks ago and I haven't been near the club since. Why would I? I've got all I need right here."

Jake just nodded thinking 'the man's delusional, that little gold digger will last only as long as the baubles keep coming'.

Jake thanked him politely and left disgusted by Moran's complete disinterest in the death of someone he'd spent hours in intimate contact with. The man was a self-obsessed tosser, Zoe was dead so what? He didn't need her any more. He had Tammy.

Glancing in his rear view mirror he saw the two of them climbing into a white Bentley Mulsanne ready to go and sample racecourse hospitality.

"They deserve each other," he muttered under his breath.

As he drove away Mo was just arriving in Aldermaston. She'd phoned earlier and made an appointment to see Anderson. She figured if she simply turned up on the doorstep he could be out and she would have had a wasted journey. She drew up outside a thatched cottage complete with white picket fence and red roses climbing up either side of the front entrance. Very twee, now who lives in a house like this? She could almost hear Loyd Grossman saying the words. 'Through the Keyhole' was one of her mum's favourite shows back in the '80s. She smiled at the thought, rang the bell and waited. The door was opened by a skinny guy, about her height with red thinning hair and a neatly clipped beard. His blue eyes framed by rimless spectacles were constantly blinking which was disconcerting and made Mo want to blink back. Managing to resist the impulse she introduced herself.

"Mr Anderson?"

 He nodded affirmation.

"DI Connolly, I rang earlier."

"Yes but you didn't tell me why you wanted to see me, just that it was important we talked. Do you have bad news? I phoned my parents immediately, thinking it might be them but they're fine so what's wrong? Why do we need this face to face meeting?"

"If I can come in I'll explain."

"Sorry, yes please do," he said, stepping back from the door.

Mo stepped directly into a small cosy living room and closed the door behind her.

"Please have a seat," he said, pointing to one of the three cottage style armchairs that furnished the room.

"Can I get you a coffee?"

Suddenly he seemed less keen to find out why she was there but Mo, determined to get the dialogue flowing, said "no, I'm fine thanks. Why don't you sit too and I'll tell you why I'm here."

He succumbed to the inevitable, sat down facing her and waited.

"I understand you know Candice, a hostess at the Blue Lagoon club?"

Embarrassed by the question Anderson turned bright red before stuttering "Candice yes I know Candice why?"

"I'm afraid that Candice, real name Zoe Dryden, was found murdered at her home in Newbury yesterday."

Anderson stared at Mo in utter disbelief.

"She can't be dead, I was with her last Sunday and she was fine. Who would do such a thing?"

"Exactly what we'd like to know and why I'm here."

"You can't think I had anything to do with it."

"Did you?"

"I would never hurt Candice, I loved her."

Mo looked shocked, of all the things she expected to hear it wasn't that.

"You're telling me you loved a woman who sold her body for sex."

"I didn't think of her that way. Look, I'll be honest, I have relationship issues with women, I don't interact well with them, I get tongue tied and nervous. Candice cared, she made me feel good about myself. I was a different man when I was with her. Yes I loved her and now I'm sorry that I'll never get the chance to tell her."

Mo saw his distress but wasn't quite convinced by it.

"You don't seem very nervous and tongue tied talking to me and I'm a woman."

He looked up at her then, teary-eyed and angry.

"Maybe you are but all I see is a police officer and an unsympathetic one at that. Your life is probably perfect, mine has just been ruined," and suddenly his whole body was wracked by violent sobs. And just as suddenly Mo believed every word.

Driving back to the station her thoughts turned to Jess and the life they shared. What made their relationship so good was because, in her mind, they were two halves of the same whole, complementary parts of life's rich tapestry, two sides of the same coin, endless poetic reasons that made them so right for each other. Unusually waxing lyrical Mo suddenly felt tears trickling down her cheeks. Crying because she was happy or crying because Philip Anderson had clearly lost the love of his life? She wasn't sure which.

Frank Hubbard was a big man and standing at 6'6" dwarfed most other men. Alan Miller at 5'11" felt as if he was looking up at a towering Sequoia and that if Hubbard spread his legs you could probably drive a car through them with space to spare. Somehow the stature of the man didn't intimidate Alan. Admittedly he was scary looking with his shaved head, broken nose and tattooed arms, but in reality his appearance contradicted the softly spoken genial giant with the ready smile standing in front of them.

"You don't look like police, more like models for Vogue," Hubbard commented, winking at Rhona.

"Flattery is always welcome but we're here on serious business I'm afraid," Miller said.

"Then spit it out, I'm a big boy now, I do serious."

The big boy reference made Miller smile in spite of himself. They were standing outside the site office and suddenly it seemed like a good idea to get a desk between them.

"Shall we take this inside?"

"Sure whatever," Hubbard said, opening the office door. He slid behind a desk littered with site maps, cardboard coffee cups and empty pizza cartons.

"Sorry about the mess," he said shrugging "but it's a building site. Pull up a chair."

Miller opened up two of the folding chairs that were stacked by the door and placed them in front of the desk. Rhona smiled at him gratefully.

Hubbard noticing asked "you two an item?"

Rhona blushed and Hubbard said "Sorry not my business."

"No," said Miller stiffly, "I think it's time we got down to the real business our reason for being here."

"Shoot."

Thirty minutes later they had gathered all the information they could and were on their way back to the station.

"What d'ya think?" Miller asked.

"He's a cheeky chappie, a man's man who likes a drink and visits prostitutes when he feels the need. Marriage didn't work out and he has no intention of walking that path again. Likes an uncomplicated life, the permanent presence of a wife would be an added complication he neither needs nor wants. Bit of a chancer but not a murderer. You?"

"I could have written that report, spot on with my own impressions of the guy. So I guess if we're right, another suspect bites the dust."

The meeting afterwards confirmed that they were no further forward. No one interviewed so far fitted the frame. Jacko had failed to identify any of the final four so they decided to call it a day.

Jake caught up with Mo just as she was unlocking her car.

"Forgot to tell you, Jess rang earlier, wanted to talk to you but you weren't back from Aldermaston."

"And?"

"Apparently she and Jaime had an interesting meeting with Kate Davis. She suggested the four of us meet up at the cottage and discuss it."

"Is Jaime there now then?"

"Yeah, want a lift?"

"I'll take my car, thanks."

"Suit yourself."

"Need it at home to get me here on Monday."

Mo opened her car door, slid behind the steering wheel of her green Mini Cooper but before she could drive off Jake folded his 6'2" frame into the passenger seat beside her.

"Changed my mind, couldn't resist the chance to have a ride in

this little beauty."

Seeing his body hunched up in the seat beside her Mo laughed.

"Even though it could be the most uncomfortable journey you've ever made?"

"Even then," he said, grinning back.

26

Kate Davis was feeling vulnerable, her partner Linda had shut up shop at 1pm and gone home; she was alone and scared. She checked all the doors for a second time and yes they were still as secure. She really was getting paranoid but the meeting with Jess and Jaime had done little to assuage her fears. More than ever she was convinced that David Mitchell was a dangerous man and could pose a real threat to her. She could identify him for God's sake and if what Jaime Summers had told her was true, he could already be involved in the murder of a woman and a child. She couldn't get the meeting out of her mind.

They arrived about 10am, leaving Linda to manage the shop; Kate took them upstairs to her apartment, made coffee and told them all she could remember about David Mitchell. Being a writer Jaime was fascinated by the so called change in Mitchell's character after the past life regression hypnotherapy.

"So can you describe this change?" Jaime asked.

"The only way to describe it is to try and explain how I felt at the time. He arrived as this polite, mild mannered, slightly nervous middle-aged man and left as an overfamiliar, arrogant, thirty something rake. Honestly, I was glad to see the back of him. After that I thought no more about it until the recording and notes were returned, then curiosity got the better of me and I Googled the guy. After discovering that Mitchell was pretending to be a dead guy I freaked and phoned you."

"Well I'm glad you did, it seems there could be a whole lot more to worry about than the fact he didn't want you to know his true identity."

"What'd mean?"

Then Jaime had explained about the murdered girl Zoe Dryden, David Mitchell's name being on her list of regular clients and the inability of the police to trace him. She remembered the look on Jaime's face when she said "more than a coincidence I'd say wouldn't you?"

This same meeting was currently being discussed in the dining room of Croft Cottage in Hermitage. Knowing Mo and Jake were on their way, Jess had prepared a plate of sandwiches in readiness. Now they were tucking in, drinking tea and David Mitchell was the chief topic of conversation.

So what'd think? Is Kate's David Mitchell the same David Mitchell you'd like to interview?" Jaime asked.

"It's a distinct possibility," Jake replied.

"Surely it's more than that Jake. Why would two guys from the Newbury area both pretend to be David Mitchell. One having undergone a complete personality transformation, the other on a list of people police want to question in a murder inquiry. They've got to be one and the same."

"I have to agree with Mo here, there's no other explanation," Jaime confirmed.

"Me too," Jess agreed.

"Okay, okay, you've got a point and I know better than to argue with three women, but Jaime put on your psychologist's hat for a minute and try to explain what's happening here."

"I'm not sure I can but I'm willing to give it a go. The guy on your list Jake, let's call him DM1, visits prostitutes. The reason he uses a false name is probably because he doesn't want anyone else to know he's visiting them."

Jaime noticed the look of 'tell us something we don't already know' pass between Jake and Mo and continued. "I know that sounds obvious but bear with me. The crucial thing here is to find out why he's bothered about people finding out. If he's married, and I suspect he is, then he doesn't want his wife to know. He must have money to afford the prices at the club, perhaps he holds an important position in the local community. If he does then he probably doesn't want his associates to know that he visits the local knocking shop. Why did he choose the name David Mitchell? I understand Jacko is already working that angle?" Jaime asked, looking directly at Jake.

"Yeah but he's getting nowhere."

"Tell him to look harder at any friends that the real Mitchell might have had. Kate Davis said that her Mitchell, DM2, was about 37, same age as the dead man had he lived."

"I'll tell him to contact the father, James Mitchell, and get a list of the son's friends."

"Descriptions too, if he can remember, it's a while ago."

"Talking of descriptions did Kate give you one for DM2?" Mo asked.

"Two actually. A before and after the hypnotherapy session, which'd want?

"Before will be fine, his attitude might change but his basic features won't."

"Well here goes then, just less than six feet tall, pale blue eyes, thinning light brown hair, mild mannered and polite."

"Ring any bells Jake?"

"Pretty well matches Cora Allen's description."

"Yeah I think we've just proved that DM1 and DM2 are one and the same man," Mo said triumphantly.

Don't put the flags out just yet Mo. Knowing that doesn't put a face to the man behind the name.

"Granted, but we do have a description and I feel if we find him we find our killer."

"Leap of faith Mo, no evidence to support that theory!"

"Gut instinct, I swear by it."

"Conjecture, pure conjecture."

"Enough, stop trying to score points and listen, you asked for my help so let me give it."

Both turned to look at Jaime, saw her exasperated expression and muttered "sorry" in unison.

Jess reached over, put her arm round Mo. "Are you two like this at work?" she asked.

"Yeah pretty much, wouldn't you say?" Mo said, smiling and looking at Jake.

"It's just our way of rubbing ideas off each other. We never dismiss anything out of hand however far –fetched and believe me Jess, your girlie has her share of whacky ideas."

"And you don't?"

"Don't start again," Jaime said, but even she was smiling now. "Getting back to Mitchell I think, as Mo said, we can now safely assume that there is only one man involved here. I remain slightly concerned about Kate, she can identify him and could be at risk. Fortunately he doesn't know she's made contact with the police, albeit indirectly through me and Jess. I do wonder what made him consult Kate, is he hoping to find something in a previous existence that will point to his behaviour in this one? What Kate didn't do, and what I think we should, is search for any information on the regression character Jeb Carter. If you believe he existed, and both Jess and I do, then he's worth a look. If you're sceptical, and I suspect you two are," she said, looking pointedly at Jake and Mo in turn, "then you probably think Carter is a figment of Mitchell's imagination. Are you up for it?"

"Living with Jess has made me pretty open-minded about all things spiritual, so I'm more than willing to give it a go?"

"Jake?"

"I'll be surprised if you find anything but, hey, give it a try."

"I'll get my laptop."

27

JEB CARTER

Two weeks ago Henry King was hung by the neck until dead at York Castle Goal. Tried and convicted for the murders of his wife Olivia and young Esme Hawkins the poor sod hadn't a hope in hell of escaping the hangman's noose. Do I care? No rather him than me.

I've moved young Grace Chandler into my cottage and moved on. She knows I can't marry her but the twenty-year-old adores me enough to forego that privilege. I'm her first lover and she's so besotted she doesn't see how badly I treat her. I haven't yet resorted to physical abuse, apart from the odd hard slap across the arse. Admittedly it makes her wince but she dismisses it as playful affection. This morning the silly bitch complained a tad after I'd subjected her to really rough sex last night, poor cow said I'd made her sore. She doesn't know the meaning of real pain yet but with each passing day I can feel the need to hurt edging ever closer. I can never get rid though; too much of a coincidence should another of Jeb Carter's women disappear.

Monkman was horrified when he found out that Grace was living here. Understandable I suppose, after all it was his granddaughter's home. There were the expected threats but in reality there was little he could do other than sack me. I know the old man doesn't like me but I've been canny and made myself pretty irreplaceable. I've been using my spare time wisely learning about the right crop rotation patterns to optimise the yield from his land. No, he won't sack me, I'm too valuable. So he'll suffer the indignity and quietly seethe.

Must get to work, time to dig trenches and plant the main crop, seed spuds. I walk into the kitchen intending to tell Grace I'm leaving but seeing her bending over cleaning the range. I'm powerless to resist the tantalising movement of her prominent arse. She's completely unaware of my presence as she busies herself black leading the grate. I step behind her, lift her skirts up above her head, pull down her drawers and enter her doggy style. Startled by the suddenness of my assault she tries to pull away. Angrily I grab her tits, pull her backwards until I'm sure she can feel every inch of me buried deep inside her. Then I begin to thrust, pinching her nipples in rhythm, harder and harder until I finally climax and collapse against her. I can tell she's crying, I don't care, she's mine to take wherever or whenever I feel the need. Straightening her skirt and replacing her drawers she turns towards me, a hurt look in her tear-filled eyes.

"Why'd do that Jeb? I told you how sore I was."

"You think I give a shit? Tell me, why'd think you're here?"

"Because you love me?"

"Love you? Don't make me laugh. I haven't loved anyone since that bitch Ginny cheated on me. I made sure she paid the price too."

She looks frightened. "What'd mean paid the price?"

Before I could tell her the door bursts open and Richard Monkman stands there, shot gun raised, pointing right at me.

"Yes Carter tell us what you mean by she paid the price? Don't even think of lying, we found the bodies."

Before I can answer I hear the gun fire, feel the impact and now as I lie here, my life slowly ebbing away, all I'm aware of is the bitch screaming and then nothing.

28

I can't believe how easy this was. No preliminaries, no polite offers of a drink, straight upstairs to the bedroom and straight to the point, demanding to see the colour of my money and a condom before she succumbs to the inevitable. I show her the money, lay it down on the bedside table and produce a pack of three from the pocket of my jeans. She undresses slowly, her eyes never leaving my growing interest and then finally naked she sinks back onto the king size bed.

"Are you joining me?" she asks seductively. Suddenly I feel is if I'm the lead stud in some low budget porn film, the seductress lying there naked urging me on onwards. I shake my head to clear the vision and hear myself saying "be patient I've something I need to do first." In one swift movement I remove the cable tie from my pocket, lean over, pull her arms above her head and secure her wrists. She barely has time to take a breath never mind react. Now, suddenly feeling vulnerable, the seductive voice deserting her she almost screams "what the hell are you doing?"

"Just making things a little more interesting. Now hush or I'll have to gag you too."

She brings her arms down in front of her and starts biting at the tie, kicking out with her legs hoping to connect with some part of my unprotected body. "You sick bastard, untie me now."

"Natalya, Natalya , you women never learn, when I say hush I mean hush."

I move toward the head of the bed away from her flailing legs and removed the bum bag concealed beneath my hoodie. It contains everything I need to restrain and subdue my victim.

She resorts to yelling obscenities and I watch as she desperately tries to shuffle her body to the end of the bed. Time for me to act. I reach over, roughly pull her bound hands back above her head and drag her back towards the slatted headboard. She's strong and struggling so I'm forced to hit her hard rendering her helpless long enough for me to secure her wrists to the head board with nylon cord. Fully conscious again she begins to scream so I force a balled handkerchief into her mouth and cover it with duct tape.

I look down at her, see the terror in her eyes and smile. She starts to thrash about again.

Bending down, brushing my lips against her cheek, I whisper in her ear. "This is my fantasy Natalya, I'm gonna fuck you whatever. So you have a choice, keep still and make it easy on yourself or struggle and I'll make it even more uncomfortable for you. Which is it to be?" She stops struggling.

I undress quickly, flinging my discarded clothes in a heap on the floor beside me. Annoyingly my fingers fumble with the condom wrapper making me curse. Taking a deep breath I finally manage to remove it from its packaging. I watch Natalya watching me as I roll it over my swollen member. Pure hatred has replaced the fear in her eyes serving only to urge me onwards. Kneeling between her legs, I force them apart, at the same time slipping my hands beneath her buttocks and raising her upwards, allowing me to enter her unyielding body. Feeling the resistance I push harder, making her stiffen muscles and increase the tension. Ignoring the resistance, I begin to pump rhythmically forcing her to relax or suffer internal injury. She relaxes making it easier and I increase the tempo until with one final thrust I shudder and collapse on top of her. I ease myself out of her body; carelessness now could result in leaving behind incriminating evidence. I stand up, remove the condom, tie the neck and drop it into a polythene bag to dispose of later. I turn my back on Natalya, big mistake; she aims a well-placed kick to my back almost making me lose my balance. Angrily I turn towards her, taking care to step out of range of her flying feet. "So you want to play rough eh? I like rough too." I hit her hard with my open hand leaving an angry red imprint on her pale face. "Rough enough for you?" Without another word my fist connects with her solar plexus causing her to curl up her legs in a futile attempt to protect herself. The pain of the blow brings tears to her eyes and also the realisation that her real ordeal is about to begin. I'm rock hard again, no fumbling this time as I tear a second condom from its wrapper and make myself ready. She's asked for rough and rough she's gonna get. She's still half dazed by the blow, making it easy for me to push inside her. Kneading her breasts, riding her hard and seeing the fear in those baby blue eyes makes me climax quickly. This time I know there'll be no well -placed kicks. She's learnt her lesson. I clean up for a second time, glance at my watch, see it's almost 2:30pm and decide it's time to end this brief encounter. I pull on my Y-fronts and can almost hear my bitch of a wife haranguing me for not buying designer pants. I smile knowing that her nagging days are well and truly over. The cow stepped over the line when she cheated on me and for that she's paid the ultimate price. I digress, this is no time for distractions. Natalya thinks I'm leaving, a look of relief washes over her. "Sorry to disappoint," I explain as I sit astride her. Pinning her body to the bed with my legs, I grab her throat, squeeze firmly until she lapses into unconsciousness. I squeeze harder and she dies. Natalya's no longer open for business, time to shut up shop. I take out the small leather pouch with its purse string closure and my suture kit, push the pouch inside her and begin to stitch.

29

"Listen to this," Jaime said excitedly and began to read out an article she'd found in a popular online encyclopaedia.

James Edward Bardolf Carter (Jeb) 1856-1887.

Carter, a farm worker from Stanton in the North Riding of Yorkshire, was thought to be responsible for the deaths of one man and three women in the years spanning 1884-1887.

The bodies of his wife Jane and her lover Frederick Simmons were found buried close to Carter's farm cottage on May 25th 1887. The bodies were discovered by another farmworker, Abraham Fletcher. On learning of the discovery Richard Monkman, farmer, land owner and Jane Carter's paternal grandfather, shot and fatally wounded Jeb Carter.

Several months before the shooting Henry King was tried, convicted and executed for the murders of his wife Olivia and kitchen maid Esme Hawkins.

A silver locket identified as belonging to twenty-three-year old Esme Hawkins and a necklace thought to be the property of Olivia King, were found at Carter's cottage. This evidence and the discovery of the other bodies points to Carter being the man responsible for their deaths.

Henry King was convicted on purely circumstantial evidence and went to the gallows protesting his innocence. He was granted a royal pardon in 1895.

Richard Monkman, convicted of manslaughter, died on 5 September 1892 in Northallerton Prison.

"What'd think of that then?"

"Told you Mitchell's our man, find him and we find our killer," Said Mo, unable to help herself.

"Granted it's odd. Carter actually existed and Mitchell somehow believes he's Carter's re-incarnation. Carter killed women, does it really follow that Mitchell's our killer?"

"Not set in stone. But facts are beginning to point the finger. The timing's right and the killing took place after the session he had with Kate Davis. As you said, he claims to be the re-incarnation of this Jeb Carter, a man who, as we've just read, is a suspected killer. We know Zoe was a prostitute, Mitchell visits prostitutes. Maybe he's a fantasist just looking for a reason to enact the dark thoughts he's been harbouring. He may have read about Carter and decided to play this game with Kate, hoping to convince himself that Carter is his nemesis. Kate said he seemed to undergo some sort of personality change, transformed from middle-aged mild mannered misfit to confident arsehole. She was intimidated. He's a good fit Jake, granted not a certainty, but a good fit."

"The worrying thing is that if Mitchell is your man he may not stop at Zoe. He could believe he's taken on Carter's mantle and with it the responsibility to continue killing. Keep all lines of enquiry open for sure but, like Mo, I think find Mitchell and you've found your killer," Jaime agreed.

"Yeah, I get all that but why did he pick Zoe? She was obviously

his choice of partner at the club so why kill her?"

"Any number of reasons, an easy target, a fantasy, maybe he's always dreamed of killing her, jealousy. Maybe he's a misogynist desiring her but hating her at the same time. You'll have to find him to find your answer."

"And therein lies the problem, David Mitchell doesn't exist. Mike Long and his men found no evidence to identify the man behind the name, so now I guess we rely on him turning up at the Blue Lagoon and Cora tipping us the wink. But why would he go back there? If he's guilty he'll be expecting us to be watching the place anyway."

"Darling don't be so pessimistic, it's unlike you to have such a defeatist attitude."

"Jaime's right Jake, think positive. Be sure, we will catch the bastard."

"Yeah you're right. I think it's this business with the boy that's really got to me. Zoe didn't deserve to die but the kid, no one should get away with killing a kid."

"He hasn't got away with it and he won't, you'll make sure of it," Jaime said, slipping a comforting arm round her husband's waist. "Let's go home. It's Sunday tomorrow, a day to chill and forget all about police work, us time."

They took their leave and as Mo and Jess stood waving them off Jess suddenly said "we need to talk."

Mo turned to look at her, worried by the tone of her voice. "That sounds serious."

"It is, so listen up Babe, we'll get dinner ready and after we've eaten, we're going sit down and discuss something that's been on my mind for some time."

"You're worrying me now, just spit it out. Why do we have to wait until after dinner?"

"It's nothing to worry about, I just want to get dinner over, relax with a glass of wine and have a meaningful discussion with the woman I love, okay?"

No amount of badgering on Mo's part could dissuade Jess from her purpose and it wasn't until they took their wine through to the sitting room and relaxed onto the sofa that she finally found out exactly what Jess wanted to discuss.

"I want to get married and I want to have a baby, what'd think?" Jess blurted out.

Mo was gobsmacked; they'd mentioned getting married at some point but a baby; where had that come from? Then she realised; of course Jaime was pregnant and it was obviously making Jess feel broody too. She set down her glass took Jess in her arms.

"Then let's get married and have a baby. Just one small point, in case you haven't noticed I don't have the right equipment to make you pregnant."

"You don't?" Jess said laughing, "then we'll have to think of another way won't we? Seriously though, you're not against the idea?" She asked, pushing Mo back far enough to watch her reaction.

"Seriously, nothing would make me happier," She pulled Jess back into her arms.

"I love you Mo Connolly," Jess whispered against her cheek.

"Me too Babe," Mo whispered back, discussion over for the evening.

30

Mo heard the church bells ringing, she was dreaming about weddings, Jess walking down the aisle on Jake's arm carrying a bouquet of white roses, while a heavily pregnant Jaime threw rose petals in their wake. The image faded as the ringing became more persistent. Bloody 'phone's spoiled my wedding day was uppermost in her mind as she rolled over to answer it. She picked up and grumpily said "yes?"

"Connolly, it's Cora Allen, you told me to ring if I thought of anything that could help, before you ask I haven't. I'm just worried, another girl failed to show last night. It was Saturday night, the club was buzzing, none of the girls miss Saturday it's the most lucrative night of the week."

"Slow down Cora, who didn't show?" said Mo, fully awake now.

"Natalya, Natalya Birinov."

"The blonde bombshell with big blue eyes, looks like Michelle Pfeiffer?"

"That's her."

"Got an address?"

"Hang on."

Mo could hear Cora opening drawers and shuffling papers.

"Found it, Dereham Street number 26."

"Okay, I'll get round there and check as soon as and don't worry Cora, she probably just wanted a night off."

"I am worried Connolly, our Russian can be a bit of loose cannon.

I've warned her so many times about entertaining clients outside the confines of the club. She's come in a couple of times nursing black eyes but she won't learn. It's all about the money with Natalya, she's always open to an offer. "

"I'll make a note of that," Mo chuckled.

"Thanks for trying Connolly, but today you can't cheer me up. Just get out there and find her safe and sound."

"I'll do my best, get back to you as soon as I know something."

"Make sure you do," Cora said, before ringing off.

Mo put her mobile down and glanced at the clock on the bedside table. God it was early, only insomniacs were awake at 7:10am on a Sunday morning. She pulled back the duvet but before she could move an arm slid round her naked body and a sleepy voice whispered in her ear. "Going somewhere? Think again, I've got plans."

Mo turned and smiled lovingly at her soon-to-be other half.

"Good news is I've just been dreaming about you, bad news is I'll have to take a rain check on those plans Babe. Cora phoned, another girl failed to show at the club last night. Have to check it out, sorry."

"Pity," Jess said, nibbling Mo's ear.

"Enough lady or I'll have to arrest you for obstructing a police officer in the execution of her duty."

Jess held out both arms in front of her, "better cuff me then."

"You're impossible."

"But you love me."

"True, but I've still gotta go," Mo said kissing her cheek, swiftly jumping out of bed and heading toward the shower.

"Need me to wash your back?" Jess shouted after her.

Fifteen minutes later she was dressed and ringing Jake.

Jaime picked up and when she heard Mo's voice said "not again please. It's Sunday, breakfast in bed followed by mad passionate sex day, tell me it's not work."

"Its work, is he there?"

"Yeah he's just walked through the door, buck naked carrying coffee and croissants."

"Too much information," Mo laughed.

"It's Mo, its work and I'm pissed off," she said, handing Jake the phone.

Jake smiled at Jaime and shrugged.

"Sorry darling, you married a cop and unfortunately they don't do a 9-5, 5-day-week. I suppose your sister's feeling pissed too."

"We're the Mason sisters, we'll get over it," she said smiling and then poking out her tongue at him.

Taking the phone he said "Mo?"

After hearing her news he simply said "yeah pick me up we'll go together and Mo, bring gloves and overshoes we don't want to incite Mike Long's wrath."

"I'd already thought of that," she said laughing "let's hope we won't need them."

"Let's, but I'll ring Mike anyway, he may want in at the beginning if there's a problem."

"Good idea, I can do without him flying off the handle again."

31

Thirty minutes later they were in Mo's Mini heading towards Newbury and Dereham Street. It was Sunday, it was early, neither one of them felt chatty so the journey seemed endless. Dark grey clouds billowed in the sky threatening rain and just before they arrived outside number 26 the first few spots began to fall.

"Talk about adding insult to injury, now the bloody heavens are about to open," Mo swore.

"Yeah and what's more I'm crammed in here like a sardine in a can, we should have brought my car." Jake grumbled.

"What a pair of grouches, neither of us want to be here, we want to be home sharing a quiet Sunday with our partners and, to top it all, we're worried about what we're gonna find. But hey, we're here now so let's just get on with it," Mo said, climbing out of the car.

Jake clambered out of the passenger side and stretched to ease his cramped muscles. Mike Long's transit van pulled in behind them and Long and two of his techies got out.

"'Bout time you got yourself a decent car Connolly, making the Guvnor travel in that tin bucket is tantamount to torture."

"Fully restored classic car in racing green making you green with envy eh Mike?" Mo quipped back, sticking her tongue out at the stocky Yorkshireman.

"Yeah, have to admit your old man did a great job restoring it but jealous, never. If I got into that thing with my girth you'd need a can opener to get me out again," Long smiled, patting his rounded stomach.

"Called out on a Sunday and still cheerful, I'm amazed," Jake said, continuing to stretch.

"Boys were jumping around on the bed, Mrs was tetchy so glad to get away from it actually. More than I can say for grumpy and grumpier there, completely ruined their Sunday so it seems."

Jake recognised the two lab techs, both were young and neither looked happy to be there. But when Mike called they had no choice but to come running.

"So how do you want to play this Mike? We have no idea if anything's amiss, just Cora Allen's gut instinct at work again. I suggest we knock and if there's no answer we'll take it from there. Okay?"

"Sure, if it's deemed necessary to go in we'll suit up then."

They walked to the door and Mo rang the bell, they waited. She rang it again still no answer. The rain was getting heavier, her short hair was plastered to her head and she could feel the water running down her neck.

"I think we need to get in Guv, after Zoe we don't really have a choice. I'll check at the rear of the house. We may get lucky, there could be an unlocked door like at the Dryden gaff."

"Don't forget the gloves," Mike Long shouted after her as she disappeared through the side gate.

She came back quickly.

"Kitchen door securely locked, damn it! There's an open window, downstairs loo probably, it's frosted glass, but much too small for any of us to get through."

"Okay Josh you're on, get us in," Mike said to one of the young lab techs.

Josh opened the bag he was carrying took out a leather kit case and removed two tools. After donning latex gloves he set to work on the lock.

"Watch and learn," Long said proudly, "this guy could be a professional burglar."

Mo watched fascinated when moments later the tech named Josh pushed open the front door.

"Glad you're one of the good guys Josh," Jake said, clapping the young guy on the back.

"How'd you do it so quickly?" Mo asked.

"Easy really, good tools and lots of practice. I can teach you if you like."

"No, you're all right thanks, one expert at the station's enough but I'll call you if I ever lock myself out."

Jake, chomping at the bit, having heard enough banter said, "shall we get on with it?"

After suiting up they searched the ground floor. All doors from the hallway into the downstairs rooms were shut and the rooms themselves in pristine condition, nothing out of place, not an unwashed dish in sight. Almost clinically clean.

"Nothing to see down here," Jake said, before following Mike Long upstairs. They found Natalya Birinov naked in the master bedroom, her wrists still securely bound to the slatted headboard.

"I'll phone Freddie, he's half expecting the call. I told him earlier we could have a problem. Josh get barriers outs front and get the stairs taped off and Ross, get busy in here." Mike Long moved onto the landing took out his mobile and made the call.

Jake could hear him telling the pathologist what they'd found, the technicians were busy doing what they'd been instructed to do and Mo was standing by the bed looking down at the body.

"Even in death she's still one gorgeous woman," she said, turning to look at Jake. "Just like Zoe, it looks as if she's been strangled and the weirdo's done the stitching up thing again, what's with that?"

"No idea, but it's got to be of the utmost significance to the bastard that did it."

Mike Long came back into the room and told them that Freddie Saunders was on his way.

"We'll wait downstairs; see what he has to say before we go."

"Appreciate that Guv, gives us room to get on with gathering evidence, if indeed there's any to gather."

Jake noticed that Long didn't look hopeful.

Downstairs in the kitchen Mo was first to speak.

"We need to get uniform involved Jake, get someone stationed outside and others knocking on doors. The suburbanites should be home so let's get talking to 'em."

"Who's on duty?"

"Joe Walsh is on the desk today, I'll get him to organise back up."

"Agreed. Two murders in a week, we need to be worried. I doubt he'll stop now and at that rate there's not much room for escalation. We need all the help we can get."

Mo phoned Walsh and gave the thumbs up to Jake.

"He's sending Dobbs and Cummings in their patrol vehicle to do door to door and they're picking up young Dawson from the station to do front of house. He's told them all to report here first for further instructions."

"Good. Mike Long just answered the door so it looks as if Freddie's here too."

"Did I hear my name mentioned?" Freddie asked, poking his head round the door. "Pity you can't get these buggers to commit crimes

9-5 Monday to Friday Jake, Sunday should be a day of rest."

"Yeah, if I had my way they wouldn't commit crimes at all. But that's living in cloud cuckoo land."

"Better get upstairs and take a look, good to see you both again, shame about the circumstances."

"Tell me about it Freddie," Mo said to his departing back.

The cavalry arrived 20-minutes later, Dobbs and Cummings were sent on door to door reconnaissance with one objective, as Jake put it.

"Find out if anyone was seen going to or coming from number 26 at any time on Saturday." Young rookie Dawson was put out front to stop any unauthorised access to the property.

"Am I getting old or does Dawson look like a schoolboy?" Mo asked after they'd left.

"Both."

"Thanks, you could have lied," she laughed.

"At least you're still cheerful," Freddie Saunders said, as he came back into the room. "Now to the serious business, rigor's still apparent which means she probably died less than 24-hours ago. Stomach contents should give us a more accurate picture. She was strangled and stitched up just like the other victim but, unlike her, she was also subjected to violence and possible rape. As well as the bruising you would expect from strangulation, she has bruising to her left cheek, to her midriff and to the inner thighs. The suturing was probably done post mortem so the MO is much the same. However, this girl was restrained and gagged and shown no mercy."

"Escalation big time, the bastard," Mo said, through gritted teeth.

"I'll get the body down to the morgue and deal with it as soon as. Hopefully tomorrow, if time allows. See you then and be prepared for a marathon session," he said, turning to leave.

"If you could PM the two women first I'd be grateful," Jake said. "Not that the boy is unimportant, but I don't think he was a target, just a casualty of being in the wrong place at the wrong time."

"You've got it, but I need to get off now, wife's cooking a Sunday roast."

"My God, how could he think about dinner after witnessing that?" Mo said after he'd left.

"Because it's just his job and he still has to eat."

"The time of death ties up with what Cora told me on the 'phone. Natalya was at the club on Friday night till late and didn't turn up on Saturday night, which gives us a window of around 36-hours unaccounted for. Shall I ring Cora or do you want me to go to the club?"

"Probably best to do it face to face, she won't need to formally identify the body cos you've already confirmed it's Natalya Birinov. But we do need to know if there are any next of kin either here or in Russia that need to be contacted."

"Cora may not know."

"Granted, but ask anyway otherwise it could mean someone spending hours tracking them down."

"By someone you mean Jacko?"

"Probably, but I don't really want to add to his burdens, I think he's got enough on his plate right now."

"I'll see what I can do. Cora does keep good records so maybe, just maybe she'll have something on Natalya. You off home now?"

"Yeah, unless you want me with you?"

"Wouldn't dream of keeping you away from your pregnant wife for any longer than absolutely necessary, besides you might do the same for me sometime soon."

Jake gave her a puzzled look. "What'd mean?"

She tapped the side of her nose conspiratorially. "All in good time, Jake."

"Well if you insist on being mysterious. I'll say our goodbyes to Mike Long and see you tomorrow. We'll need a get together before we go to the morgue so don't be late."

"Bloody cheek. I'm always in before you." She laughed, went to the front door stripped of her white suit and shouted "thought how you're getting home?" Opening the door she saw it was still raining. "Nice day for a walk."

He ran out into the hall and said "oh sod it, I came with you didn't I?"

"Yeah I'd forgotten too, no alternative then you'll have to come to the club first."

"Okay, give me a minute to talk to Mike and I'm ready to go."

Five minutes later they were on their way to see Cora Allen.

32

Mo phoned ahead to say they were on their way and Nick Danvers told her he would leave the side door unlocked so they could go straight in.

True to his word Nick had left the door open and as they went in they could here Scarlet's flawless voice rehearsing Peggy Lee's iconic version of 'Fever' drifting through the bar.

You give me fever, when you kiss me

Fever when you hold me tight

Fever in the mornin'

A fever all through the night

Nick spotted them immediately and put his finger to his lips. Understanding they stood and waited until she finished the song. When she did they both applauded loudly and she stood and bowed to her audience.

Unable to stop herself Mo blurted out, "that was beautiful, you're wasted here you know."

"You're so wrong Connolly, I love Cora, I love this place and I get an appreciative audience every time I perform. I'm a big fish in a small pond; out there I'd be a small fish desperately trying to stay afloat in a sea of talent. Which would you rather be?"

"Point taken, but I still maintain you have the talent to appeal to a much wider audience."

"We love it here, it's right for us, we're staying put," Nick confirmed.

"Glad to hear it," Cora said, joining them in the bar. "So Connolly, if you've finished trying to steal my staff away I can only assume you and your handsome boss are here with news of Natalya and from the look on your face it's probably all bad. Is she dead?"

"Yes, I'm so sorry."

"Me too. She had her faults but she was still one of my family here and we'll miss her, won't we?" she asked, looking directly at Nick and Scarlet Danvers.

As they nodded their agreement Mo noticed the tears forming in Scarlet's eyes.

Nick wrapped his arms round her and said, "rehearsal over, I'll take you home."

"You'll be okay?" he asked Cora.

"Fine, I'll see you tomorrow."

"Ok, if you're sure."

"I'm sure; after all I'm in the protective custody of the police now."

After they left Cora locked the door behind them.

"You two want coffee upstairs? You must have questions to ask and I have some of my own."

"Sounds good to me Ms Allen."

"Call me Cora, I allow all good looking men that one privilege."

Jake had to smile. Cora Allen still showed resilience in the face of adversity and he had to admire her for it.

"Okay thanks Cora, we gratefully accept your hospitality."

"Even the great Jake Summers succumbs to flattery," Mo whispered as they followed Cora to the lift that would take them up to her penthouse flat.

"Make yourself comfortable," Cora said, pointing to one of the sofas as they entered the sitting room. "How do you take your coffee Jake? I may call you Jake?"

"You may and I take my coffee black, no sugar."

"Why am I not surprised?" she said, winking and heading for the kitchen.

"She's flirting with you and you're lapping it up," Mo sniggered.

"Don't be ridiculous, she's old enough to be my mother."

"So, she's still flirting with you," she said, playfully punching his arm. "Seriously, how much do we tell her?"

"Everything, if he's targeting girls that work here then she needs to warn them for their own safety."

"Warn who?" Cora asked, returning carrying a tray bearing three coffees and a plate of assorted biscuits.

"We'll get to that soon, first sit down and let's explain what's happened," Jake said in such authoritarian way that even Mo shot him a warning look.

Cora's eyes flashed with anger. "I'm not stupid Jake, ask Connolly there. I know that Natalya's been murdered probably by the same arsehole that killed Zoe and if that's true then he could be targeting my girls. Right so far?"

"Right," he answered, taken aback by the vehemence in her voice.

"Right, then don't pussyfoot around me, just tell it as it is."

So he did.

"We're not releasing the fact that he stitches his victims up, it's probably his signature and we don't want or need any copy-cat killers out there muddying the waters so we would appreciate you keeping that snippet of information to yourself."

"Yeah I get that but what's his motivation?"

"We have a couple of theories but they're just that, theories, so I can honestly say at this time we don't know why he does it. Just tell your girls to exercise caution, not to let anyone into their homes, even men they might know from the club."

"I'll tell them, but like Natalya some of them are motivated by money and may ignore my warning."

"If they choose to ignore it and anything happens then you will, at least, have done your best to protect them," Mo said sympathetically.

"Did Natalya, like Zoe, have regulars?"

"No, she didn't have a client list. There are always new punters at the club and she liked variety, so she wouldn't see anyone more than twice. She didn't want anyone getting too close, a strange girl in many ways. Most women have at least one good friend but Natalya didn't, she was a loner, lived for possessions not people."

"Do you know if she had any family?" Mo asked.

"Said her parents were dead but who knows, you couldn't always rely on her being honest. She definitely had a half-brother though, used to brag about him all the time. He worked at the Russian Embassy in London. About 12-years older than her, married with kids and she seemed to adore the whole family, always taking time off to visit. When he found out what she was doing, that was it, all contact stopped, end of fraternal friendship. She hadn't seen him for well over a year, never spoke about him again so he could have moved on."

"Do you have a name?"

"I think his Christian name was Andrei and she always said he was from her father's first marriage so I guess his surname was Birinov too, but I can't be sure."

"Thanks, that's great. One other thing before we leave, did she seem unduly worried about anyone, a punter, a stalker, maybe a sense of being followed, anything at all really."

"She did joke about some young guy who lay in wait for her every Saturday morning outside the gym on Park Road. Apparently he'd been brought to the club for his 21st by his brothers, they ate here and then they paid for him to share an hour or two of Natalya's time while they enjoyed themselves with two of the other girls. The boy was well and truly smitten and kept pestering Natalya for a date. Dating a 21-year-old that wasn't her style, she didn't do relationships and he was far too young anyway. He was persistent though, turning up every Saturday hoping she would change her mind but she never did. Secretly I think she was flattered though she'd never admit it."

Now, their police antenna completely tuned in, they were both leaning forward in their seats listening intently as Cora gave them this interesting information. Jake was the first to respond. "Did he ever threaten her?"

"I don't think so, as far as I know he was just a young lad with a crush."

"I don't suppose you got a name?" Mo asked hopefully.

"Natalya called him Mark, Mark Forster, no Forrester, Mark Forrester."

"Brilliant, well done Cora you've just given us another avenue to explore."

"Glad I could b be of help. Any luck locating Zoe's sister?"

"Yeah, our in-house computer whiz found out their surname, the company he worked for and they were able to give us an address in Cornwall. We got in touch with the local police and they sent a family liaison officer round to the hotel to break the news. The family are on the way home now so we'll be round to see them tomorrow."

"Poor Diana will be devastated, they were close, Zoe told me."

Mentioning Zoe brought Cora close to tears again so Jake stood.

"Thanks again Cora, we'll be in touch and let's hope in better circumstances."

"You don't need me to identify Natalya then?"

"No, fortunately DI Connolly did that at the scene."

"Of course, you knew her."

"Never formally introduced, but yes I knew her from the club. From the information you gave us it shouldn't be too difficult to locate the brother and get him to the morgue to back up my initial identification."

"Well at least I'm spared that," Cora said, sounding relieved. "I'll come down and let you out."

33

"Where to?" Mo asked, as they fastened their seat belts.

Home I think. Not much more we can achieve today. We need to gather our thoughts, gather the troops and go from there. What'd think about Forrester?"

"Well he's on the radar, he's someone of interest but honestly, like Cora said, a boy with a crush. My money's still on Mitchell. You?"

"Infatuated, rejected, definitely worth a look but the big sticking point for me is Zoe. If he was a frequent visitor to the club I'd be happier, but he wasn't so it's unlikely he knew her. Why would she let a complete stranger into her home? Doesn't make sense does it?"

"Agreed, so question him but keep our options wide open."

"That goes without saying. Tomorrow's going to be hectic. I'll get Jacko tracking Andrei Birinov, he needs to be told about his sister's death. We need to attend the Post Mortems, talk to Forrester and get in touch with Diana Preston and all that after the meeting. I feel exhausted already."

"Best get you home quickly so you can rest up in readiness then. A baby on the way too, the burdens a DCI has to bear. If only you were a young man eh?" she joked.

"What was that Sergeant?" he joked back.

"Very droll. You can't demote me, I'll deny all knowledge."

"Changing the subject Mo, I'm going to ring Helen Davis tomorrow.

Two deaths, undoubtedly the same offender, so potentially a serial killer on our hands here. She won't be happy but she needs to know."

Jake thought of Helen Davis, the Assistant Chief Constable of Thames Valley, as his mentor. She was the reason behind his transfer to Newbury from the Met. They'd worked together at the Met and she'd targeted him for the Newbury post when the previous incumbent, DCI Chris Burton, had tragically died in the middle of the Price investigation. Five women had already died by the Coffin Killer's hand before Jake and his team prevented a sixth victim from suffering the same fate. He remembered the ACC saying afterwards "I knew I'd picked the right man for the job" but he knew only too well that the boss is only as good as the team that support him. He looked over at Mo and smiled 'and who better than her' he thought.

"What you thinking about?" Mo asked.

"Things."

"What things?"

"So much has happened in my time here."

"None of which would've happened without me," she laughed. "Let's face it, you met your wife through me, I helped you catch a serial killer, and now I'm going to help you catch another. I didn't help with the pregnancy but, hey, that just one small detail."

"Then I owe you my heartfelt thanks Connolly, I doubt I could exist without you in my life," he said sarcastically.

"Just as long as you appreciate that Guv and, by the way, you're home," she said, pulling into his driveway.

"Do you want to come in for a drink?"

"No thanks, I want to get off before Jess sends out a search party and anyway, according to Jaime you have unfinished business to attend to."

"Bugger off then, I'll see you tomorrow," he said, struggling out of the car. Once upright he started stretching again.

Watching the performance Mo leaned over the passenger seat and said "I take it you won't be wanting a lift then?"

"On your way Connolly," he replied, before slamming the door shut.

He stood on the driveway and imagined her smiling face as she drove away.

He found Jaime in the kitchen.

"Good you're home, I was beginning to think I would spend all of Sunday alone."

"You have my undivided attention for the rest of the day," he sniffed the air. "Whatcha cooking?"

"Chocolate Cake, I had a fancy for it, there was none in the house so I'm making one."

"Great stuff, there's only one thing I love more than chocolate cake."

"What's that then?"

"You of course," he said, drawing her into his arms for a long and meaningful kiss.

34

Mo put her key into the lock but before she could open the door it was flung open by an excited Jess who, slamming the door behind them, dragged her into the Kitchen.

"I've spent the day reading about our options."

"Calm down Babe, you've lost me. What options?"

"Our baby options, for having our baby."

"Oh, so nothing important then," Mo joked.

Jess gave her a playful punch on the arm.

"You! I just didn't realise so many options were available to us."

"Well how about I take a shower then we can go into the sitting room and you can tell me all about what's on offer."

"I've got a better idea, forget the shower for now, I'll make tea and then we'll talk."

"You got it," seeing Jess all fired up how could she refuse.

A few moments later she was sharing Jess's baby fervour.

"So our options are these; we could find a sperm donor and go the turkey baster do it yourself route. We could go to a clinic; they would provide sperm from a known or an anonymous donor and do the insemination. Or we could do the partner to partner egg sharing thing."

"What's the egg sharing thing?"

"It's becoming very popular amongst same sex couples."

"Yeah but what is it?"

"It's a procedure that would allow both of us to be involved. The biological mother provides the eggs which are fertilised by donor sperm and then implanted into the birth mother. So when the child is born it really does feel as if it belongs to both of them. If the sperm donor is anonymous then that ensures he will play no further part in the child's future. So no added complications further along the line. What 'd think?"

"Sounds perfect, I provide the eggs and you have the baby. Now, give me the bad news, how much?"

"Expensive, but here's the sweetener. If you're under 35 and allow other women to use your frozen eggs, that would go a long way to offset the cost of treatment. I can't imagine you being bothered if there were a few little Mo Connollys running around." "You're really up for this aren't you?" Mo laughed.

"Yeah, I really am."

"Then let's go for it, but I'd like to make an honest woman of you first."

Jess threw her arms round her. "Then let's gets married as soon as possible and get this show on the road. I can't wait to tell Jaime."

35

MONDAY

Determined to be early Jake left the house at 8am. Wall-to-wall slate grey clouds filled the sky and promised rain yet again. Feeling miserable because of it, he cursed out loud "bloody weather, dismal start to another bloody dismal day". Then he squared his shoulders and thought 'grouch, be positive things can only get worse' making himself smile and feel better about the day ahead. By the time he left Jaime was already at work in the den. She'd promised to let Jackson Fielding, her Literary Agent he'd have the first draft of her new book 'Abyss of Darkness' by Friday. Distracted by Jake's new case she was behind schedule and needed to knuckle down and finish it. She was a stickler for meeting deadlines and this one wouldn't be any different.

Jake arrived at the station at exactly 8:22am. Mo must have heard him arrive, she was standing in the doorway of the 'boardroom' looking at her watch. "Afternoon Guv, we're in here."

He walked over popped his head round the door and was embarrassed to see that everyone had arrived before him, including the uniformed officers DI Leyland, Dobbs, Cummings and Dawson. Even Mike Long was there. He took Mo by the elbow and steered her out of their hearing.

"How long have they been here?" he whispered.

Honestly, our lot about 5 minutes, uniform a couple of minutes before you arrived and you're early this morning," she grinned. "After your comment yesterday I had to prove a point didn't I?"

"I should have known better Connolly, a throwaway comment from me turned into a challenge you couldn't resist. Now I'm finally here let's get on with it shall we?" he said, placing his hand in the small of her back and propelling her forward at speed.

Before they reached the door she twisted away. "Before we go in Jake, we've already been inundated with calls from the press so I've organised a press conference for 3:30pm, gives us breathing space to do the things we need to. As you said, it's gonna be a busy day."

"3:30pm sounds fine. Newshounds always amaze me, they seem to get information almost before we do."

"Pre-requisite of the job, they have to be born sniffing."

The room quietened as they took the two remaining seats at the head of the table.

"I won't apologise for being late 'cos I'm not, but I do appreciate the fact that you're all here so we can start promptly." The statement, as intended, produced a ripple of applause.

"I expect by now you've all heard that yesterday another dead body was discovered at an address in Newbury. The dead woman, Natalya Birinov, worked at the Blue Lagoon club and was undoubtedly a victim of the same man that killed Zoe Dryden. Freddie Saunders did a preliminary check at the scene and confirmed she'd been strangled and probably died between 11am and 5pm on Saturday. Hopefully he'll be able to pinpoint it more accurately after he completes the Post Mortems later today. However, unlike Zoe this victim was tied to the bed and her body showed signs of violence and sexual assault but, again, we should know more later. Cora Allen told us that some young guy, a Mark Forrester, had been pestering Natalya, hanging around asking for dates that sort of thing. He's 21, probably local and has twin brothers. They all went to the club a few weeks ago to celebrate Mark's 21st. Jacko, I'd like you to locate him as soon as and then Dusty, you and Rhona pay our Mr Forrester a visit. DI Connolly and I will be attending the PMs so now hopefully I can sit down and Inspector Long will tell us what was found at the scene."

"One word Guv, nothing. My guys dusted the whole of the upstairs for prints and nothing, so he either wore gloves or wiped everything before he left. My guess is the latter 'cos we only got her prints on things inside the bathroom cabinet. We took photographs before the body was moved and afterwards we looked for signs of sexual assault. Again nothing, no bodily fluids identified so I guess if he did rape her then he used a condom. The cable tie and nylon cord used to tie her to the bed are commonplace and can be bought from any DIY outlet. Not very helpful but that's it I'm afraid."

"Thanks Mike. I'm not surprised, you didn't sound hopeful yesterday. Now door to door, any luck lads?" Jake asked, focusing his attention on Dobbs and Cummings.

Officer Dobbs took it upon himself to be their spokesman.

"We might just have got lucky here Sir." Taking out his notebook began to read. "Mr. Matthew Docherty aged 32 of 29 Dereham Street, which happens to be directly opposite number 26, reported seeing Natalya Birinov arrive home around 11am Saturday morning in a bloody nice motor." The young cop blushed, "his words not mine, Sir, but to continue he said it was a red Mercedes convertible and he even remembered the personalised number plate Far1. Said Ms Birinov was accompanied by a young guy, the driver, who was wearing jeans and a hoodie. They went into the house together. The car was parked outside for at least three hours, he didn't see it leave but said it was still there at 2:15pm when he left his house to go shopping."

"Could he describe the man?"

"No Sir, he had the hoodie pulled over his head but Mr Docherty assumed he was young because of the clothes he was wearing."

"Did anyone else see him?"

"No Sir, unfortunately he was the only one in the street who could help with us with our inquiries. We did check the number plate through ANRP (Automatic Number Plate Recognition) and the car belongs to a Samuel F Farraday of Newnham Gardens here in Newbury. He's a 50 year-old businessman, owns Farradays on the Industrial Estate, they make and fit bespoke oak kitchens."

"Thanks fellas, you've done a great job. Dave, Steve, get round there after this meeting and see why Mr Farraday's car was parked outside 26 Dereham Street on Saturday."

"Yeah, but before you do disappear come and see me. I want to hear how the Jamieson inquiry's coming along," Mo interrupted.

"Well if there's nothing more let's get on with it."

Jacko raised his hand, "just to let you know I still can't trace Mitchell or any of the other guys who gave false names."

"Not to worry Jacko, if you can't find them no one can. We'll just have to rely on a getting a break. We think the punters we've checked on so far are just that, punters. None of them fit the frame for this, Mitchell's the one we want to take a closer look at. For now concentrate your efforts on finding Forrester, Dusty and Rhona are relying on you. Oh yeah, I almost forgot, Cora Allen's pretty sure Natalya had a half-brother, some sort of diplomat at the Russian Embassy in London, an Andrei Birinov. She hadn't been in contact with him for a couple of years so Cora has no idea if he is still there. So Dusty, Rhona check it out while Jacko works on Mark Forrester. Okay guys, let's get on with it." Jake looked over to Barry Leyland. "A word before you go, Barry."

Barry Leyland got up and as the others left he sat down beside Jake. "Sir?"

"Just wanted to say thanks for your cooperation and ask if you could make Dobbs and Cummings available if we need them. They seem bright lads."

"Of course, Sir. So not satisfied with stealing Halliday, you want Dobbs and Cummings too?" Leyland joked, but Jake thought he could detect a note of sarcasm in Barry Leyland's reply.

"Come on Barry, we both know I didn't steal Halliday. There was

a vacancy in CID for another DC and he applied and got the job."

"Just joking, Sir," Leyland said, looking uncomfortable under Jake's scrutiny.

Jake just raised his eyebrows and said, "I'm about to phone ACC Davis, she's always happy to know that CID and uniform are collaborating to solve an important case."

At the mention of Helen Davis, Jake watched Leyland snap to attention suddenly sitting bolt upright in his seat, his ruddy complexion suddenly ruddier and his military moustache visibly bristling.

"Always happy to work with CID, you know that Sir."

"So we're good Barry."

"We're good Sir."

As he left Jake smiled knowingly. Mention anyone higher up the food chain and Barry Leyland wanted to impress.

He left the 'boardroom'. He passed Mo's office, she was still talking to Gregg and Halliday so he went into his own, closed the door and picked up the phone. Helen Davis was in a meeting so he left a message with her secretary.

A moment later Mo wrapped on the door, he looked up and beckoned her in.

"Just been catching up on the Jamieson case, no progress I'm afraid. There's been no sighting of the car involved. Uniform are keeping their eye open but unless it's found we might never find the culprit. I've told Gregg and Halliday to take a closer look at Paul Jamieson and his alibi. Call me cynical, but he could have been having an affair with his secretary and she could be complicit by providing the alibi."

"Definitely cynical Connolly, but if you've got a gut feeling run with it. I trust your gut instincts Mo, but the world's not full of men cheating on their wives so be prepared for disappointment. Changing the subject, are you ready for the mortuary experience? Two messages while we were in the meeting, one from Diana Preston, she's home and would appreciate some information and Freddie phoned, he'll be ready to start the PMs in 30 minutes or so."

"My day just gets better," Mo said, grimacing, "you wanna go now?"

"Don't want to but yes, we'd better go now. Freddie won't be happy if we keep him waiting."

36

Feeling totally drained Jake glanced at his watch it and sighed. They'd just arrived back at the station after a very long morning at the mortuary. They'd spent almost five hours there while Freddie went through the motions, photographing the bodies, taking tissue samples and basically confirming what they already suspected; that both victims had been strangled. In addition to the blunt force injuries found on their necks, pin-point haemorrhages on the skin and in the eyes were further evidence of asphyxiation produced by strangulation. Natalya had also suffered a fracture to the hyoid bone. Genital bruising, tearing and internal examination confirmed that she had also been raped. Freddie had taken swabs but wasn't hopeful they'd produce any DNA evidence. The one interesting discovery, apparent only when Freddie removed the stitches, was the leather pouches that had been pushed inside each of the women's bodies. Inside each pouch was an old gold coloured twelve sided thrupenny piece.

"What'd make of that then?" Freddie asked.

"Impossible to say but I know a woman who might have some idea," Jake said, immediately thinking of Jaime.

"Then I'll leave it with you to discover its significance, if indeed it has any. I think we're finished here."

They left the mortuary, both grateful it was over and finally they could breathe fresh air.

***

His head was throbbing, the smell of formaldehyde mixed with equally pungent disinfectant lingered in his nostrils and it was 2:35pm already. Less than an hour to gather his thoughts before the fourth estate descended upon them, complete with cameras and unanswerable questions. He sighed again.

"What's up Guv?"

"Just thinking, the bloody press will be here in less than an hour. What do I tell 'em?"

Then as they walked into the squad room, as if a prayer had been answered, he spotted Helen Davis talking to Miller. Jake walked over towards her beckoning Mo to follow.

"Good to see you Ma'am."

"You too Jake," she said, shaking his outstretched hand. "Good to see you too Inspector Connolly. I got you message Jake, I've just been quizzing DS Miller here, seems you have a problem. How can I help?"

"Well as you're here and asking Ma'am, we have a press conference scheduled for 3:30pm. I would be grateful if you could front it."

"Let the three of us go to your office and you can bring me up to speed then."

"I'm not up to speed myself Ma'am, we've only just arrived back from the mortuary so I haven't had time to liaise with my men."

At 3:20pm they emerged from Jake's office with a plan to keep it simple. Helen Davis, true to her word, spoke to the gathered reporters.

"We're here really just to confirm that the bodies of three people have been discovered at two addresses here in Newbury. The deaths do appear to be related. An inquest will take place on Wednesday when the victims will be formally identified and cause of death determined. DCI Summers is in charge of the investigation team and the police are actively pursuing several lines of inquiry. Thank you for your attention."

And then the questions were fired from every direction as they moved to leave.

"Is it true that the victims are prostitutes working out of the Blue Lagoon Club?"

"No Comment."

"Was one of the victims a child?"

"No Comment."

"Does one live on Dereham St?"

"No comment."

Edging closer and closer to the door and being pressed on all sides, Helen Davis was losing patience.

"Ladies and gentleman, we have nothing more to say at this time so please just let us get on with the job of finding the person or persons responsible."

Reporters being reporters weren't easily dissuaded but hearing the determination in her voice they stepped back and allowed them to leave without further hindrance.

"Thanks for that Ma'am, at least they had the good grace to relent in the end."

"Contradiction in terms Jake, good grace from the press never, they just realised further information was not forthcoming."

"I'm going to have a catch up session with my squad now. Do you want to sit in?"

"Love to, unfortunately I need to get back, another meeting I'm afraid but keep me posted and remember I'm just a phone call away. Good to see you both again."

She left them at the stairs and picked up her driver at the front desk.

"Nice lady," Mo commented, as they made their way upstairs.

"None better," Jake agreed.

"Good she was here to deal with that mob, with my thumping head I would probably have lost patience." As they walked into the squad room Jake said "gather 'em up Mo and let's see if there's anything to smile about."

He walked into the 'boardroom', sat down and waited. Immediately he noticed photographs of the three victims already pinned to the board and assumed that Mike Long had provided them. Looking at the photo of young Zak Dryden made him feel helpless and angry. Poor kid, hardly had time to experience life and now he was dead, killed for being in the wrong place at the wrong time. Miller and Grey were the first to arrive and the rested drifted in over the next few minutes. Last to arrive was Mo. She closed the door behind her, sat down next to Jake and passed him a glass of water and a box of Aspirin.

"Formaldehyde, does it every time," he explained, taking out two pills, throwing them into his mouth and washing them down with a gulp of water. "Thanks Mo, you're a life-saver."

"Guv."

"Okay, Dusty you first, did you find Forrester?"

"Well Jacko managed that for us, we just followed up on it. Mark Forrester works at the Newbury and Crookham Golf Course, he's part of the green keeping team. Apparently he also shows promise as a player and working there gives him plenty of opportunity to practice."

Miller, noticing Jake drumming his fingers on the desk, quickly got to the point. "Not important really Guv, just giving you a bit of background on the guy. Anyway that's where we found him. He readily admitted that he was infatuated with Natalya and that he had made a regular Saturday morning pilgrimage to the gym on Park Road with the hope of persuading her to go out with him. He spoke to her briefly last Saturday but as usual she blew him off. Then comes the really interesting bit, as she walked away from him he noticed a red Mercedes Convertible pull up alongside her. She obviously recognised the driver, walked over to the car and after a brief conversation got into the passenger seat and they drove off. He described the man as old, about 40 with thinning sandy hair and he also thought the guy was wearing a navy hoodie but couldn't be sure."

"Remind you of anyone, Guv?" Mo asked.

"Mitchell."

"Yeah, yet another pointer in that direction I'd say. We've just gotta find the bastard."

"I'd just like to add Guv that both Rhona and I think that Mark Forrester is an innocent in all of this, he's just a young guy with a crush."

"I don't doubt that for a moment Dusty, that's ruled him out for me too. What about Andrei Birinov? Did you manage to track him down?"

"Well Rhona did so I'll hand over to her."

"Andrei Birinov is still on the current diplomatic list at the Russian Embassy. He's listed simply as an Attaché no clue as to what he's responsible for or linked to. I phoned a contact in the Met told them the situation and they will break the news to Birinov. Doubtless we'll be getting feedback at some point. That's it for now Guv."

"Thanks Rhona, now we just need your report," Jake said, singling out Gregg and Halliday. "And please Gregg, I've got a headache so none of your Cockney rhyming slang. Eh?

A ripple of laughter went round the table making Gregg feel embarrassed so he turned petulantly to Halliday and said "you do it."

Chuffed, young Steve Halliday didn't need to be asked twice. "We met with Mr Samuel Farraday at Farradays on the Thatcham Industrial Estate. He was astonished that his car was seen in Dereham Street on Saturday. Said he parked it in his usual bay when he got to work at 8:30am and it was still parked there when he left at 5pm. He has at least five witnesses to confirm that. Apparently, although he owns the place, he often works alongside his men on the factory floor and that's exactly what he did on Saturday. So there's no way he drove his car to Dereham Street, or anywhere else for that matter. He said that our witness, Mr Docherty, must have been mistaken about the number plate. We checked with PC Dobbs who said Docherty was adamant it was correct because it was personalised and therefore easy to remember. Oh, Farraday did say he left a spare key taped to the underside of the front offside wheel arch. He went to check and it was still in place, but it also means that if anyone else knew about it they could have borrowed the car and returned it again before it was missed."

"Did you ask him who knew about it?"

"We did Guv, and he just said too many to remember."

"Brilliant, has so much money he doesn't care that his Merc could so easily be stolen. Okay, well done guys. The Mortuary was as usual the worst place in the world to be. The two women, like everyone suspected, were strangled. Natalya Birinov was battered and sexually assaulted and, bizarrely, both women had their vaginas stitched up. Even more bizarre was the fact that when the stiches were removed, Freddie Saunders found that a leather pouch containing and old thrupenny bit was pushed inside their bodies. Doubtless significant to the killer, but you need to be a psychologist to get inside their screwed up heads. That information stays in this room, am I clear?"

They all nodded their agreement.

"Can I just say something before we leave Guv?" Dave Gregg piped up.

"Be my guest Dave, take the floor, you have our undivided attention."

"Well I know Cockney slang may get on your nerves, but it may be just the thing to shed light on the significance of the coin found inside the bodies."

"Go on."

"Those old thrupenny bits were made of brass and that's slang for prostitute. Brass nail is rhyming slang for tail, which in the 19th century was a word for a prostitute. More than that, thrupenny bits is slang for tits, so we have tail and tits and thrupenny bits. Probably means he thinks of these women as nothing more than cheap tarts, in other words worthless women who deserve to die."

Jake and Mo both sat with their mouths open totally gobsmacked. Mo was the first to react. "Well done Dave, you may well be on to something there."

"Well done indeed," Jake seconded. "Definitely something to think about, thanks for that."

"Does that mean I can use it freely now then?"

Mo was quick to answer. "Definitely…. not, you explaining the meaning is great, but using it in everyday speech you might as well be speaking Chinese."

"I take it that's a no then," Gregg said grinning.

"With a capital N Dave," Mo said, grinning back.

"Good. Okay, then we'll call it a day and thanks guys, good work," Jake said, standing up. Everyone followed his lead and drifted back into the squad room.

Left alone with Mo he said, "what'ya thinking?"

"We're not really any further forward are we? Two possible suspects crossed off the list, nothing we didn't already know at the morgue and no further information on our friend Mitchell. I have this weird feeling we're missing something. I was impressed by Dave's insight, good work there but all-in-all not a lot achieved today, nothing that leads us any closer to Mitchell."

"I agree, the guys have done everything asked of them but I am still ending the day feeling slightly disappointed. Hey tomorrow's another day, we mustn't be despondent. Like you I was impressed by Gregg, still waters run deep eh?"

"Yeah, I think we may have underestimated our Dave. Finished for the day?"

"Not quite, I've got to ring Diana Preston to apologise and arrange a meeting for tomorrow, wanna come?"

"Why not? For now I'll leave you to it. It's been a long day so I'm off home to take a shower, wash the smell of the mortuary out of my hair and put my feet up."

"Great idea, I won't be far behind you. Love to Jess."

They walked together into the squad room which was virtually abandoned. Only Jacko remained, still beavering away on his computer.

"Go home Jacko, you're making the place look untidy," Mo shouted over to him.

"Soon Guv, soon," he shouted back.

Mo just shrugged and whispered "the man's obsessed, he'll give the rest of us a bad name."

Jake smiled. "I'll make sure to kick him out before I leave. See you tomorrow."

37

Prowling through the empty house like a restless tiger, need to focus, get grounded. Sitting down I switch on the TV and channel hop, hoping something will grab my attention and help me relax. It doesn't relax me but certainly grabs my attention. Meridian News carries a headliner.

'Three bodies have been discovered at two addresses in Newbury. Two women, thought to work out of the Blue Lagoon Club here in Newbury, and a child have been found murdered in their homes in the smart suburban areas of the town. Police think that the deaths are related and, according to Thames Valley Assistant Chief Constable Helen Davis, are actively pursuing several lines of inquiry. The investigation will be headed by DCI Jake Summers. It was his team that finally nailed Jonathan 'Coffin Killer' Price who was responsible for the abduction and murder of five women in Berkshire and Oxfordshire.

An inquest into the deaths is scheduled for Wednesday when the victims will be formally identified and cause of death determined. Cora Allen, owner of the infamous Blue Lagoon Club on Fenton Street, refused to confirm that both the dead women worked there. The club has long been a target for local campaigners who describe it as nothing more than a high class brothel. Police and local councillors are powerless to act because the owner runs a legitimate high class restaurant and bar and the fact that she rents out rooms to her hostesses is not an issue. She is not, as she has said on many occasions, running a brothel. What the hostesses choose to do in those rooms is entirely up to them. Accepting money for sex is not illegal. Running a brothel is. She does not accept money on their behalf, nor does she book appointments or allow soliciting in her club. This loophole in the law has allowed the Blue Lagoon Club to flourish unhindered for several years. In fact the private opinion of one councillor was that if it keeps them off the streets it's no bad thing.'

I switch off the set and start pacing again. I'm agitated, clicking my fingers as I walk from room to room, I need to think. They found the bodies but then that was always going to happen, meaningless in the grand scheme of things. They may be pursuing several lines of inquiry but they can't possibly be looking in my direction. They don't even know who I am. I begin to relax and even begin to enjoy my notoriety. The thought of the police chasing their tails, maybe hunting a man that doesn't even exist, gives me a feeling of superiority. I think of Natalya, the lovely Natalya, completely in my power and my body reacts in the only way it can. I need a woman, dare I go back to the club knowing that the police will undoubtedly centre their efforts there, or shall I cruise the district where the night slags ply their trade? Not something I relish the thought of but just to use and abuse, does it really matter? I suppose I could even try the conventional route of picking someone up in a pub but no, not sound judgement, far too many witnesses.

For now I need to relieve myself of the growing problem in my pants, time to visit the bathroom.

38

'Bliss. A quiet night in with the woman I love, in the house that I love, better make the most of it before our little family addition arrives to change our lives completely. When two become three, and who knows in the future maybe four, it will be wonderful but different, we'll never get this time again   precious us time,' Jake thought, as he stood in the kitchen watching his wife prepare salad.

Hobbs was desperately trying to attract his attention, weaving in and out of his legs purring loudly. Getting no response the large marmalade moggie stood on his hind legs wrapped his front paws round Jake's right leg and dug in.

"You hairy monster," Jake shouted.

"He doesn't like being ignored," Jaime laughed.

"I'll boot your sorry backside outside," Jake threatened, as he bent down to retrieve his leg from the clinging cat.

"He's all talk Hobbs, just full of bravado, what he'll really do is go over to the cupboard get out the biscuits and feed you."

"You think?"

"I know, you love that cat almost as much as you love me."

"Ha!" he exclaimed, but went to cupboard anyway, retrieved the cat biscuits and poured some into Hobbs's bowl.

Big green eyes followed his every move and then the cat wandered over to the bowl, gave Jake one last 'about time' look before tucking in.

"There, told you so Hobbs , he's just putty in your paws. If you weren't a cat I'd be jealous."

Later, as they sat together on the sofa watching the news reveal details of the case, Jake turned to her and said "can I just run something by you?" He told her about the coins found in the victim's bodies and Dave Gregg's theory.

"What'd think?"

"I think he's spot on. The killer does think his victims are worthless and that accounts for the naming and shaming and derogatory amount of money. Stitching them up signifies the end of their working life you can't sell sex when the venue's been closed down. Yeah, so Dave Gregg's been very perceptive."

"That worries me somewhat, Gregg being perceptive is a concept I can't quite get my head round."

"Jake!" she exclaimed.

He laughed. "Seriously though, I keep thinking we're missing something vital. Mo's convinced if we find Mitchell we find our killer and I tend to agree, but the fact remains that we have no idea who he is."

He told Jaime about Forrester seeing the guy in the red Merc, about the witness providing the number plate and the subsequent discussion they'd had with Farraday.

"Surely whoever took the car must be, at the very least, acquainted with Farraday to know where he hides the spare key."

"That's it, you're a genius," he said, leaning over to kiss Jaime on the forehead. "Give Farraday Mitchell's description and see if it rings any bells with him. Thank you, thank you, thank you. I'll have to phone Mo."

"Not tonight you don't," she said, dragging him back down beside her. Nothing can be done 'til morning anyway, let it be. I have far more interesting plans for you."

"And what would they be?" he asked, letting his body relax against her.

"I only do the descriptive in my books in real life I demonstrate," she said, nuzzling the side of his neck.

"Be my guest, demonstrate to your heart's content."

And she did.

***

At Croft Cottage Jess and Mo were also discussing the case after watching that same news broadcast.

"They already know about the women working at the Club then, no doubt the media greased a few palms to get that gem of information," Jess said.

"Yeah, I'm sure they did and then to top it all by dragging out all that business about the club and Price, pure sensationalism. They never have, nor ever will, warrant my respect."

Jess grinned at her. "Changing the subject, guess what I did today?"

Mo playing her game replied, "what did you do today Sugar?"

"I booked our wedding. The local vicar is willing to perform the ceremony and has a free slot six weeks Saturday, so I booked it. Provisionally of course, told her I'd confirm tomorrow if you agreed. So, what'd think?"

"You certainly don't let the grass grow, do you Babe?"

"Is that a problem?"

"No, I'm delighted to be swept off my feet by my decisive fiancée."

"Do I detect a hint of sarcasm? It's not compulsory, if you don't want to marry me just say?"

"Whoa where did that come from? Of course I want to marry you, I just didn't think it would be that soon. There's a lot to arrange and I'm up to my eyes with these murders, doesn't leave me much time to sort things out."

"I'll make all the arrangements, you just make a few phone calls to your family. I'll do the rest."

"Then you're on, six weeks Saturday is fine and, Jess, I am 100% committed to this wedding and us, don't ever think otherwise."

"I don't, I just thought you might be as excited as I am."

"I will be, promise. As soon as we get this maniac behind bars I'll give it my full attention."

"I can live with that and I'm sorry I got grouchy."

"I'm sorry too and, honestly, I am as happy about it as you," Mo said, leaning over to kiss her on the forehead. She looked at her watch, it was 9:30pm. "It's not late, I'll ring home now and tell them our news, gives them plenty of time to get suited and booted. I'll even ask dad if we can use the Daimler so you can go to church in style," she said enthusiastically. Mo's father, Ed, restored classic motors, particularly MG sports cars. Jess had seen the 1951 red Daimler convertible that Ed had so lovingly restored from a beat up rust bucket to a thing of sheer beauty that he hired out for weddings.

"Fabulous, now that's the enthusiasm and excitement I wanted to see," Jess said laughing.

The phone rang just as she was about to pick up.

"Perhaps they're ringing us, now wouldn't that be a coincidence," she said, reaching for the phone.

"Connolly?" Cora Allen almost whispered down the wire.

"Yeah," Mo replied, a feeling of dread washing over her. What the hell had happened now? Surely not another no show girl."

"I'm in the bar and guess who just walked in?"

"For God's sake Cora, just tell me."

"David Mitchell's just 10 feet away chatting to Lena Dosti."

"Try and keep him there, I'm on my way. I've gotta go Jess, Mitchell's at the Blue Lagoon Club."

"Not alone you're not, phone Jake and get some back up."

"No time," she said, and before Jess could object she was out of the front door and into her car.

Jess dialled Jaime's number and waited.

"Hi sis, what's up?" Jaime answered and heard the panic in Jess's voice.

"I need to speak to Jake, it's urgent."

"Okay I'll get him."

"Jess?"

"It's Mitchell Jake, he's at the club and Mo just hightailed it out of here. I'm worried Jake, she needs back up."

"Don't worry Jess, she's more than capable of taking care of herself. None-the-less, I'm on my way and I'll phone the station and get a patrol car outside now. They'll get there fast and meet up with her when she arrives."

"Thanks Jake," Jess said, feeling grateful and relieved.

He hung up, told Jaime briefly what was going down and left the house. He used the car phone to summon the troops and was pleased when Sgt Walsh said he'd send Dobbs and Cummings. The journey passed in a blur as it often does when your mind's elsewhere. He found Mo, Dobbs and Cummings inside the club. Mo was spitting feathers, Mitchell had left the club before she'd arrived and Cora in her wisdom had sent Nick Danvers to follow him.

"I could hardly detain him," Cora whinged, "he could have been armed and dangerous and I wasn't prepared to subject the club and the people in it to mayhem."

"But you were prepared to put Nick Danvers at risk?"

"Put a sock in it Connolly, you want Mitchell and Nick, just maybe, can tell you where he is or, at least, where he's heading. He won't take unnecessary risks. He spent years in the marines protecting himself in explosive situations, he's certainly up to a little surveillance work. Did you really expect me to let Mitchell just walk away? He could be the monster that killed two of my girls."

Mo had never seen Cora so angry.

"I'm sorry, that was wrong of me to assume you would put anyone at risk."

Unappeased Cora said, "yeah, it was."

The phone behind the bar rang and Cora moved to answer it.

"I think you've upset her," Jake whispered.

"Yeah me and my big mouth, but then I had no idea that Danvers was ex-army."

Cora walked back towards them with a smug look on her face. "Nick followed him to a house in Bergeman Close. Mitchell parked his car on the driveway and went into the house. Nick can't see the number but he's parked on the road outside in his blue Astra and will stay there until you arrive, making sure that Mitchell stays put. Good enough for you Connolly?" she asked sarcastically.

"Good enough Cora, I am truly sorry and thank you, at least we haven't lost him."

"Just don't doubt me in future."

"Believe me, I won't. I made a mistake, it won't be repeated," she said ruefully

39

"No point taking three cars, leave yours here Mo and we'll pick it up later. You two follow us, we may need you," Jake said to the two cops.

"Sir," they said in unison and headed towards their patrol car.

"You know where Bergeman Close is?" he asked Mo as she slid into the seat beside him.

"Yeah it's only about a mile from here, turn right out of Fenton Street then take a left onto the A339 heading South. Take the first right onto St John's Road, at the first roundabout take a left onto Newtown Road and about 250 yards, a right into Bergeman Close.

"Too much information Connolly, just tell me where and when to take the next turning."

Minutes later they arrived, spotted the Astra on the road outside a large detached property on the left hand side. There were no more than 15 individually designed houses nestled here in the leafy southern outskirts of Newbury, opposite open fields and woodland.

"Nice area," Jake commented, as he pulled up behind Nick Danvers.

"Almost as nice as the Lechampstead gaff you own," Mo joked.

They walked up to Nick's car and he wound down his window. "No movement in or out of the house so he must still be inside."

"Thanks Nick, we'll take it from here," Jake said. Nick raised his hand in farewell as he drove away. Jake waved the police car into the vacated spot and spoke to the officers through the driver's open window.

"DI Connolly and I will go to the front door and ring the bell. I want you two round back in case he tries to leg it but stay out of site if you can, we don't want to alarm him, he could be armed and dangerous."

Jake waited until Dobbs and Cummings had disappeared through a side gate to the back of the house then rang the bell.

A small dumpy woman about forty with straggly, straw-blonde hair and one of the plainest faces Jake had ever seen, opened the door. She looked him up and down.

"If you're one of those Jesus freaks, we're not interested" and went to close the door on them. He moved quickly, stuck his foot out preventing her and said "police ma'am, we'd like to speak to David Mitchell please."

"Never heard of him, you must have the wrong address," she said, again attempting to shut the door in their faces.

Jake held fast and the woman became agitated and asked him to remove his foot and allow her to close the door.

"Can't do that ma'am, a man known to us as David Mitchell was seen entering these premises less than thirty minutes ago."

"The only person who came into this house was my husband and his name certainly isn't David Mitchell. Our name is Johnson, Marilyn and Clive Johnson."

"Then we'd like to speak to Mr Johnson please, if only to confirm he's not the man we're looking for."

The woman was suddenly joined by her husband.

"I'll deal with this Marilyn, nothing to worry your pretty head about, just some sort of misunderstanding about the car. You go back inside and watch the telly. I'll talk to the officers, it won't take long."

Marilyn beamed at her husband and did as she was told.

'Even the smile couldn't transform Marilyn Johnson into anything resembling pretty,' Mo thought.

Johnson waited until she was out of earshot. "What'd want? Is it about the club? That's the only place I'm known as David Mitchell."

"Yes Mr Johnson, it's about the club. We'd like you to come down to the station and answer some questions."

"What about?"

"I think you know what about," Mo said accusingly.

"I have no bloody idea," Johnson said, becoming increasingly nervous, his pale eyes darting from side to side avoiding any direct contact with their own.

"Then I'll tell you Mr Johnson, I'm arresting you on suspicion of the murders of Zoe and Zak Dryden and Natalya Birinov. You do not have to say anything, but it may harm your defence, if you fail to mention, when questioned, something which you may later rely on in court. Anything you do say may be given in evidence. Do you understand?" Jake said.

Mo was taken aback she hadn't expected Jake to arrest Johnson, just to take him in for questioning.

Panic replaced nervousness and made Johnson belligerent. "What the bloody hell are you talking about? I haven't murdered anyone. So I've dipped my wick in a prostitute or two, that doesn't make me a murderer."

'You horrid little man,' Mo thought, and suddenly she was overjoyed that Jake had arrested him.

Having overheard the outburst Marilyn Johnson ran into the hall slapped him across the face and shouted hysterically. "Dipped you're wick have you, you bastard."

"Hardly surprising is it with an ugly bitch like you waiting at home."

Now he really was showing his true colours but Marilyn was a match for him.

"With a dick like yours you probably had to pay double for the privilege, you wanker," she screamed, waggling a little finger under his nose.

Johnson raised his hand and Jake reacted quickly, grabbing his arm to prevent him striking her.

The commotion brought Dobbs and Cummings running. "Cuff him, put him in the car and we'll see you back at the station," Jake said.

"Yes cuff the bastard. Once you get him in a cell keep him there and Clive darling don't rely on me for an alibi. I'll just tell them the truth, you're never at home," Marilyn Johnson screamed, as they led her husband away.

40

Under the street lamp she'd looked almost pretty but the harsh reality, now she occupied the passenger seat of my car, at close quarters she was far from pretty and certainly not as young as she first appeared. She had the haggard and careworn face of a middle-aged woman who'd spent a life on the streets supporting her pimp and an equally expensive drug habit.

So what's it to be darlin' a blowjob for £20?" she said, bending her head towards me. "Or we can climb in the back and I'll give you the works for £50."

I almost wrinkled my nose in disgust. "Neither sweetie, I'm looking for an all-nighter in a nice comfortable bed. I'm willing to pay £400 for the privilege. You have a place where we won't be disturbed?"

"£400? Can't afford to turn that down can I? No funny business though, no bondage, no beating, just straight sex yeah?"

"Yeah," I agreed, "so where we going?"

"I share a flat with a mate on Kitchener Street by the canal, you know it?"

"Yeah I know it, but I didn't sign up for a mate or an audience."

"Then you're in luck. Soph's working Reading this week, won't be back 'til Saturday so we've got the place to ourselves. No audience, I promise," she said with a girlish giggle. "If she'd been here you could have had us both for £400."

"Now there's a thought," I say smiling.

"Let's go then darlin', get this show on the road. I'm Roxy by the way, known as Foxy Roxy in the business."

"David," I replied.

"Nice to do business with you David."

I was pleasantly surprised by the apartment. It was clean and tidy with an open plan living area, integrated kitchen and two bedrooms both served by the bathroom that separated them.

"This one's mine," she said, opening the door to the bedroom on the right of the bathroom. It was furnished with a double bed, a dressing table and a large oak wardrobe, simple and functional. The bed was made and looked clean. She saw me appraising the surroundings and said "I've never brought anyone here before, it's my sanctuary the one place that's truly mine and I like to keep it nice."

I nodded appreciatively, took out my wallet, counted out £400 and laid it on the dressing table.

"A true gentleman, doesn't need to be asked for the money, just one more thing …"

I took out a pack of three and held them up before she'd finished the sentence.

"Naughty boy, you've come prepared for a long session so we'd better get started."

She turned her back and began undressing. Again I was pleasantly surprised, her body looked good. Her small breasts, released from the bra were firm and rose tipped and her legs long and toned, not a hint of sag anywhere. 'Maybe, just maybe, I could enjoy fucking her' I thought, feeling my erection pushing against my pants.

She turned and walked slowly towards me. "I can see you like what you see," she said, glancing toward the bulge in my pants. "They're just a hindrance, shouldn't you be getting 'em off?"

"All in good time," I said, pulling her towards me, lifting her up into my arms and carrying her towards the bed.

"My, aren't we the romantic one," she giggled.

I dumped her on the bed. Turning her onto her front and forcing my knee into her back, I quickly rendered her unconscious by putting my hands around her throat and blocking the blood supply to her brain. A trick I learned many years ago when practising martial arts. She wouldn't remain unconscious for long so I had to act swiftly. I used nylon cord to tie her arms and legs to the carrying handles on either side of the mattress so she was bound spread-eagled to the bed. I wasn't prepared to suffer another kick from flailing legs. As she began to stir I stuffed a sock in her mouth and taped over it. Now she was completely helpless and at my mercy. That thought made me smile, I don't do mercy. I pulled the dressing table stool beside the bed, sat down and waited. In less than a minute she was fully awake and, finding herself restrained and gagged, was visibly terrified.

"Sorry darlin'," I said, mimicking her, "I lied about the beating and bondage bit."

Panic setting in, she started to struggle which heightened my desire. I couldn't see her face clearly in the dim light but the body sure looked inviting.

"Relax darlin' you'll hurt yourself, you're going nowhere," I said, hurriedly shucking off my clothes.

Careful as always I donned a condom, knelt between her spread-eagled legs, lifted her onto my swollen penis and rode her brutally all the while kneading her breasts and watching the look of terror in her eyes. I came quickly and collapsed against her. Giving myself a moment to recover, I lay between her legs, feeling the rapid beating of her anxious heart.

Then all business and knowing I didn't want to go there again I simply whispered "goodnight and goodbye Roxy baby," and ended her worthless life. I left her tied to the bed and literally stitched up.

41

"Nasty piece of work, our Mr Mitchell," Mo said, as they drove back to the station.

"Yeah, but I'm still not 100% sure he's our man."

"Then why arrest him?"

"Because those pale darting eyes made him look guilty and because he turned bolshie and that's another sure sign of a guilty man."

"That doesn't make sense, you think he's guilty so you arrest him and now you're beginning to question that judgement."

"Because I can't figure out why he would turn up at the club again. If he was responsible for killing two of the women that work there, why put yourself at risk that way? Unless he's completely stupid, he must have known that the police would be all over the place. It doesn't sit right."

"Maybe, but it doesn't alter the fact that all the evidence so far points the finger at him. Kate Davis can identify him as Mitchell cum Jeb Carter. Mark Forrester saw the man that picked up Natalya in the red Merc and he fitted the description that Cora Allen gave us."

"You're right, so let him sweat overnight in the custody suite, interview first thing and then get Barry Leyland to serve him with identification procedure forms. Then we get Reading or Oxford to set up a VIPER (Video Identification Parade Electronic Recording), they're both equipped with the recording facility. Hopefully both witnesses will finger Mitchell. If they do I think we'll have enough to formally charge him. You agree?"

"One hundred percent."

When they arrived at the station Mitchell was already being processed at the front desk by the Custody Sergeant, Jim Crowther. Dobbs and Cummings were standing either side of Mitchell who was emptying his pockets and removing jewellery. Crowther was busy cataloguing them and putting them into a plastic bag but looked up as they walked in.

"Sir, Ma'am, I'm about to read this fella his rights, get him fingerprinted, photographed and swabs taken. Anything more you need tonight?"

"No thanks Jim, we'll leave him in your capable hands 'til morning. We'll interview him then," Jake said. Turning to Mo he said, "I'll run you back to the club to pick up your car and then it's home, grab some shuteye and get in early tomorrow. Okay?"

Dobbs, overhearing, said "I can run DI Connolly back to the club Sir, we don't both need to be here now."

Jake looked at Mo. "Okay with you?"

"Fine, see you tomorrow."

The three of then started to move away and Mitchell shouted after them.

"I want my solicitor here now, this minute, and I'll be suing your sorry arses for wrongful arrest."

Jake turned back. "Lock him up Jim, give him plenty of time to cool his heels and calm down."

Mo had to move a polystyrene food container and an empty coke bottle from the passenger seat of the patrol car before she could climb in alongside Dobbs. "Call you away from a roadside snack, did we?" she said, smiling at the young policeman.

"No Ma'am, its Roy. He's addicted to fast food, gets grouchy if he's not topped up every three hours or so. I've warned him repeatedly that he'll be a prime candidate for a heart attack by the time he's forty, but it falls on deaf ears."

Mo suppressed a smile, wondering at the young man's earnest concern for his partner's health. Most men of his age were immune to the effects of bad eating habits. By the time they reached the club she'd had a full rundown of what Roy Cummings could consume during a shift, making her wish she'd never commented in the first place.

It was just after 1am when she arrived home and wearily walked through the door of Croft Cottage. Jess was still up and happy to see she was home and still in one piece.

"Hi Babe," she said, giving Jess a hug. "You shouldn't have waited up."

"I was worried; you flew out of here four hours ago like an avenging angel so I phoned Jake to get you some backup."

"He told me and thanks Babe. Mitchell, aka Clive Johnson, was an arse and he could have turned nasty making it difficult for me to handle him alone. Anyway, he's safely under lock and key and I'm home. Let's get some shuteye, I need an early start tomorrow."

42

TUESDAY

It was early, traffic was light and Mo was surprised to see it was only 7.55am when she pulled into the station car park. She noticed Jake's BMW immediately; he never got in before her, he must be really keen to interview Johnson. She walked into the station and spotted him at the front desk talking to Joe Walsh, who had replaced Crowther as the on-duty Custody Officer. As she approached she heard Joe saying that Johnson was already sequestered in a consultation room with his solicitor, George Merrill.

Merrill, a partner in the firm of Merrill, Oxley and Turner, was a high profile solicitor who was known for representing the rich and influential elite of Newbury. Jake was impressed. Merrill, although expensive, was the best in the business. Jake had clashed swords with him once before and knew he would be a serious sparring partner across the interview desk. Determined to make a start, Jake asked Joe Walsh to escort Johnson and Merrill to interview room 1. They had a lot to achieve in the next 16-hours or it would mean applying for a detention extension order from Matthew Parks, the Super at Reading.

They were still waiting ten minutes later and Mo could see Jake was getting more fidgety by the second.

"Merrill's trying to wind you up Jake, don't let him."

The door opened and Walsh escorted the two men into the room. PC Dawson followed them and stood inside the door.

Walsh left and before anyone could speak Merrill looked directly at Jake. "Sorry to keep you waiting Detective Chief Inspector, but I was in the middle of an important confidential discussion with my client."

Jake held his gaze. "No worries George, it's not as we've got anything better to do, now is it?" he replied sarcastically.

The remark served only to make Merrill smile.

'Smarmy bastard' Mo thought, but kept schtum. She switched on the tape, named the people present and Johnson's interview began.

An hour and half later they were no further forward. Asked about his whereabouts at the times relevant to the murders, Johnson just replied "at home with the wife." Asked whether his wife would corroborate this he said "I doubt it."

Asked why he used the name David Mitchell he said "why'd think? I didn't want anyone to know that Clive Johnson was fucking a prostitute cos his bitch of a wife never came across. Cow has cost me a fortune over the years and now thanks to you she'll probably divorce me and take the rest of it."

"Why'd choose the name David Mitchell specifically?" Mo asked.

"I knew him at school, poor sod got killed a few years back. Just thought it was kinda nice to think of him enjoying himself posthumously. Nice touch eh?"

'You sick bastard, if you were so meek and mild you certainly went through a personality change after seeing Kate' Mo thought. However she followed up by asking "you're not denying that you knew Zoe Dryden and Natalya Birinov?"

"Why would I? Candy, or Zoe as you call her, was my first choice whore, I like the dark haired and doe eyed ones. Saw Natalya at the club a few times but she wasn't my type."

So if we tell you we have a witness who saw you pick up Natalya Birinov in a red Mercedes convertible on the morning of her death you'll deny it?" Jake asked.

"Too bloody right I will, never been near the woman. Anyone telling you otherwise is lying," Johnson said angrily.

"Calm down Clive, the police obviously have no evidence to place you at either scene so I guess that means we're free to go, am I right Detective Chief Inspector?" Merrill said, patting his client soothingly on the back.

Jake, completely ignoring Merrill, looked at Johnson. "So Mr Johnson, if you're as innocent as you say you are you won't mind taking part in a video identification parade?"

Before Merrill could stop him Johnson said "bring it on and then you won't mind if I sue your sorry arses for wrongful arrest."

Jake nodded to Mo. "Interview terminated 9:55am," she said and switched off the recorder.

"PC Dawson will escort you back to the Custody Suite and Inspector Leyland will be along shortly to give you the identification procedure paperwork, then we can get that underway, okay?"

Merrill gave Jake a filthy look. "It will have to be, my client has already agreed to it on tape."

Jake was very temped to do a one up sign but instead said "nice to see you again George," and under his breath "you miserable bastard."

As soon as they went upstairs Mo rang Reading to organise the ID and Jake was immediately called over to Jacko's desk.

"I heard about the arrest Guv, just wanted you to know that James Mitchell couldn't identify this fella Johnson as one of his son's friends. Like he said, if the guy was a casual acquaintance or someone David knew from school or work then he probably wouldn't know him anyway."

"Thanks Jacko, good try but Johnson's already admitted knowing David Mitchell at school, knew he was dead and that's why he used the name."

Mo came over and confirmed Reading was on the case. "We should have a video line-up of mug shots ready in a couple of hours, so how about we spend the intervening time speaking with Diana Preston?"

"Good idea, see if she's available and we'll go in about 30-minutes. I just want a brief catch up with the guys, keep them up to date with what's going on."

"Okay I'll check," Mo said, striding back to her office.

Jake gathered his squad together in the 'boardroom',, waited for Mo to appear and then told them what had led to Mitchell's arrest, the subsequent interview and the VIPER that had been organised with Reading.

"When we get copies of the mug shots I want Dusty and Rhona to see Kate Davis and see if she can identify Johnson, and DI Connolly and I will see Mark Forrester. Jacko, keep plugging away with those other descriptions from Cora. I presume you two are still working the Jamieson case?" he asked, looking at Gregg and Halliday.

"Yeah Guv, in fact we were off to see Paul Jamieson when you called us in, so unless you want us working anything here that's where we're going," Gregg said.

"I thought you were seeing him yesterday?" Mo said, surprised.

"So did we, but we couldn't locate him. Wasn't at work, wasn't at home, didn't know where else to look so we left a message with his secretary to get in touch when he turned up for work, which she did this morning."

"Okay, better get over there before he disappears again," Mo said, "and Dave, make sure you talk to the secretary too."

"Already did and honestly there's no way she'd be having an affair, she's a plump 60-year-old, has a brood of grandchildren and talks about them non-stop. We don't see her as anybody's bit on the side, do we Steve?"

"Not a chance," Halliday replied, looking embarrassed.

"We've probably drawn a blank there Guv, the guy looks clean. I certainly don't think she'd lie for him."

"Even so take a closer look Dave, just pull his chain a bit."

"You're the boss."

"Let me know how it goes," Mo called after them as they left the squad room.

"Dave's not happy with you," Jake whispered.

"Like he says, I'm the boss. He'll get over it."

"Still got a gut instinct about Jamieson?"

"A niggle, nothing more."

"Changing the subject, is Diana Preston free to see us."

"Yeah, she's at home all day."

"Then shall we?"

"Let's," Mo said, following him out.

43

Sophie Edwards opened the door to the flat and was surprised to see that the place appeared empty.

"You still in bed you lazy cow?" she shouted, fully expecting Roxy to stagger out of the bedroom. "I'm putting the kettle on for a brew, Roper brought me home, the bloody pimp told me I was wasting my time and his money. One miserable client last night, that's all I managed and he was a bloody pensioner. Paid me twenty quid for a blow job, didn't even cover the cost of the B and B. I tell you Rox, I swear the whores of Reading have a monopoly on the trade there. Are you hearing me lady?" she said, flinging open Roxy's bedroom door. And then she screamed.

Jake got the call just as they were about to leave the Preston's house. The meeting with Diana Preston had been a harrowing experience. The woman was understandably distraught, unable to accept that her sister and nephew were both dead and probably even harder for her was the knowledge that Zoe had sold her body for sex.

"She didn't have to, you know, she could have stayed here helping with the children. It was working well, we were happy to have her but Zoe wanted her independence. If I'd known how she planned to earn it I'd have tried to talk some sense into her."

Seeing the woman so upset and, in an attempt to appease her, Mo said kindly "she wasn't planning to make it her life's work you know. According to Cora Allen, the owner of the Blue Lagoon, all Zoe wanted to do was earn enough to give Zak a good life and to support them while she finished her degree. Then she would get out there and make her mark in the legitimate workplace. Zoe was a good person, just a mother determined to do the best she could for her son and she certainly didn't deserve to die, never forget that."

"Thank you for that," she said, giving Mo a hug. "You're right of course. Now all I have to do is come to terms with it. When will be able to give them a decent burial?"

"The inquest will be held tomorrow and after that the bodies should be released for burial," Mo replied.

"Let me know when you catch the monster that killed her won't you?" she said, tears spilling from her red-rimmed eyes.

"Of course," Jake said standing to leave. "And again, we're sorry for your loss."

They shook hands with her and as she shut the front door behind them Jake's mobile vibrated in his pocket.

"Hang on, phone's going off and I better take it," he said, touching Mo's arm.

"Summers." Then it went quiet and Mo saw a look of disbelief wash over his face. "You're kidding right? Where the hell is Kitchener Street? Okay we're on our way."

"Jake?"

"That was Mike Long, there's been another one, young woman about 25, name of Vicky Bennett also known as Roxy, lives in a flat on Kitchener St. Flatmate found the body when she arrived home this morning. Same MO as the others, step further this time though. Apparently the bastard stitched up her mouth too."

"Do we have a time frame?"

"Freddy's there now, let's get over there and find out."

"I'll drive," Mo said, "one of my friends used to live on Kitchener Street so I know it well."

When they arrived the flat had already been taped off and young Dawson was keeping dog eye.

Mo smiled at the young PC. "You seem to be making a habit of this Dawson."

"Not through choice Ma'am, you coming in?"

"That's why we're here," Jake said abruptly.

"Sorry Sir," Dawson blushed.

They ducked under the crime tape, pulled on protective suits and went inside.

"What was that all about, Jake? The kid was only asking."

"I know I'm sorry, it's just another body turning up now just when we think we've arrested the culprit."

"It depends on the time of death, he could still be in the frame. It was after 9pm when he turned up at the club last night."

Forensic techs were busying themselves in every room and Mike Long was deep in conversation with a young dark haired woman who was sitting on the sofa looking pale and nervous. He turned when he heard Jake's voice. "This is Sophie Edwards Sir, she shares the flat with Vicky Bennett, the dead woman. She hasn't seen Vicky since Monday but tells me she spoke with her on the phone about 6pm yesterday. Sophie arrived home at 10:15am this morning, found the body and called the station."

"Ties in nicely with my preliminary examination," Freddie Saunders said, coming out of what presumably was the dead girl's bedroom. I'd say death occurred between 7-11pm last night. Outwardly looks to be the same MO, some escalation, know more when we do the PM. I'll get the body picked up as soon as possible."

"Thanks Freddy, we'll be in touch," Jake said, shaking the pathologist's hand.

"Mike, DI Connolly," Freddie said, nodding to the two officers as he left.

Mo walked over to Sophie Edwards and sat on the sofa beside her.

"Sophie, I'm DI Connolly. So can you tell us if Vicky had any regular clients here at the house?"

"Roxy you mean, she's always been Roxy to me."

"Okay, did Roxy have regulars?"

"I dunno, how would I? She works the streets same as me but we never bring Johns home. This is our place, we keep it nice and never sully it with sex."

"So where do you go with clients?"

"Mostly do what needs to be done in their cars, sometimes cheap hotels. Dunno what she was thinking bringing him here. Must have been a good little earner for her to break the house rules."

"She didn't say anything on the phone then?"

"Only that she was going out later to try her luck."

"Okay Sophie thanks, I think that's all for now. Do you have somewhere you can go until forensics finish up here?"

"Yeah I'm going home, stop being a rebel and get myself a proper job like my mum always hoped I would. She'll forgive me in time and after this I'm more than happy to suffer the sharp end of her tongue."

"Where's home? We'll probably need to talk to you again."

"Mum lives in Hungerford, Temlpleton Close, number 9. I'll be there if you need me."

"Do you have transport?"

"Yeah, got a little clapped out Fiat, parked out back."

"Roadworthy I hope."

"So the MOT tells me."

"Okay you're free to go. And Sophie, don't come back eh?"

"You've gotta be kidding. After what happened to Rox they'd have to drag me back here screaming and shouting. No believe me I've had a wakeup call, I won't be back."

After Sophie left Mo joined Jake who was talking to Mike Long.

"Did you get the gist of that?"

"Yeah, basically she can't help."

"The one good thing to come out of this mess is it's made her rethink her lifestyle choices."

"Another dead body and hallelujah she's found salvation, not much consolation is it?"

"Brutally cynical, as usual, Guv."

"Realistic Mo, but I'm glad you at least can draw comfort from a saved soul."

Long laughed. "You make Connolly sound like a ministering angel, in reality she's probably the toughest cookie on the force."

"Believe me Mike, if you think that you don't know our Mo at all. She doesn't often show it but she's one of the most compassionate people I know."

Mo felt herself blushing. "Enough," she said. "I'm standing right here you know."

"You've made Connolly blush Guv, that's got to be a first."

Mo gave Mike Long a drop dead look and Jake winking at him said, "timely exit in progress before we have another dead body to deal with. Be sure to tell us if you find anything useful. Let's go Connolly, we've got things to do people to see."

She couldn't help grinning as she followed him out.

44

"Mike's never forgiven me for trashing his crime scene. Or is that really how he sees me, the toughest cookie on the force?" Mo asked, as they drove away.

"Don't be daft, he doesn't hold grudges he was just ribbing you. Mike always likes to take the mickey," Jake said, laughing at his little joke.

"Very droll." And because it made him laugh, she couldn't help laughing too.

When they arrived back the video-fits were ready. Dusty and Rhona had already left to see Kate Davis so they grabbed a quick coffee before driving over to the golf club to see Forrester. Traffic was heavy due to road works on the B3421 so instead of the usual three minutes it took nearer 20 to reach the golf club.

"We could have walked here in fifteen minutes," Jake grumbled, as they got out of the car.

"Maybe, but then you'd have moaned about carrying the equipment and how it would have been so much easier to drive."

"You make me sound like a persistent grouch."

Mo just looked at him and raised her eyebrows making him grin.

They went to reception and asked to see Forrester. A pretty young woman in her early twenties wearing a name badge that read Georgie Adams beamed at them when his name was mentioned, making Mo immediately think 'this is a girl with a massive crush on Mr Mark Forrester'. And 5-minutes later, when he turned up at the desk, she understood why. He was tall over 6-feet with blonde tousled hair, a well-muscled physique and handsome in a youthful Brad Pitt kind of way.

He asked Georgie if it was okay to use the office behind reception. Would Georgie have said no? Never in a million years. They showed him the mug shots which he looked at carefully. He hesitated when he came to Johnson.

"This could be him, I can't be 100% sure as I only saw the guy at a distance".

He looked at the remaining faces and turned to Jake. "Number seven is the only one that bears any resemblance to the guy driving the Merc. Unfortunately I can't possibly provide a positive ID, sorry."

"Not to worry, thanks for your help anyway. If anything at all jogs your memory and you think it can help please get in touch," Jake said, standing and shaking the young man's hand.

"I was hoping for a positive ID, not enough there to give us a reason to hang onto Johnson. Let's hope Dusty's having more luck.

Kate Davis was having another look at the faces that made up the video identification parade. On completion of the second run through she turned to Dusty. "Sorry he's not there, number seven is the only one that vaguely resembles Mitchell. Similar pale blue eyes but the guy here has a fuller mouth, the shape of his face is different and he has more hair and it's also a couple of shades darker."

Rhona, visibly disappointed, asked "you're absolutely sure?"

Kate was adamant. "Absolutely, I was closer to him than I am to you for well over an hour. The guy in the video could be a relative, but it's not David Mitchell."

On the way back to the station Rhona was unable to mask her

disappointment.

"I was convinced we had the right guy but it seems we're back to square one. If a man who admits to calling himself David Mitchell isn't the David Mitchell we're looking for, who the bloody hell is?"

"DC Grey, language!" Dusty laughed. "Don't wind yourself up, perhaps the Guv had better luck."

"I doubt it. If Kate Davis didn't pick him out then we don't have a hope in hell with Forrester."

They drove the rest of the way in silence, both lost in thought.

They arrived back and seeing their glum faces Jake didn't need to ask how it had gone.

"That's it then," he said, "we've got to let Johnson go. No reason to keep him here any longer."

"Looks like it Guv, Kate Davis picked out Johnson as a lookalike but was adamant the man was not David Mitchell," Miller explained.

"Exactly the same result as we got. Forrester hovered over Johnson's mug shot but was unable to give us a positive ID. Bugger it, I really thought we had him. Johnson's a bastard but not our bastard, so it seems. Dusty, go downstairs and get Sgt Walsh to release him."

Jake turned to Mo. "Expect the shit to hit the fan now, the bastard's bound to sue us for wrongful arrest."

"I'll slip downstairs and remind him about the threatening behaviour he exhibited towards his wife and how that won't go down well in the divorce court. Also, the world will find out his real name and the fact that he likes to frequent brothels. I think I can persuade him to go quietly."

"You're a true gem Mo Connolly. I'll leave it in your capable hands."

"Remember that true gem analogy when you do my annual appraisal report," she said, before disappearing out of the squad room.

'I won't need to remember, I'll have you to remind me when the time comes,' he thought, and the thought made him smile. Mo Connolly really was his right hand man.

Fifteen minutes later she was back and poking her head round Jake's door. "He left huffing and puffing but he won't give us any trouble."

"Thanks, that's one thing less to worry about. Come in, shut the door and sit down."

"Sounds ominous," she said, complying.

As she sat down Jake said "where do we go from here Mo? We were both convinced that if we found Mitchell we found our murderer."

"Me more than you Jake, you always had a nagging doubt."

"What's happening here Mo? We've obviously got two guys both calling themselves David Mitchell. Why?"

"I can't answer that but the fact that both witnesses hovered over Johnson's mug shot makes me wonder if, in fact, the two could be related."

"Yeah, that's something I've been mulling over too. Should've asked Johnson before we released him."

"That would've proved pretty pointless Jake, he was in no mood to cooperate."

"Granted, but we could've tried. I feel we've let him go and he probably holds the key to solving this case."

"Get Jacko on the case, see if Johnson has brothers, cousins, whatever, you can bet he'll find them."

The phone rang and Jake picked up. Mo gathered from the one sided conversation that the press had found out about Johnson's arrest and subsequent release.

Eventually he slammed down the phone. "Did you get that?"

"Press Office?"

"Yep, they're being badgered by the nationals and local TV for a statement. They've heard about the arrest so now they're demanding to know if we've charged anyone in connection with the murders."

"Guess that means another bloody press conference."

"Already arranged by the press office, we've got a couple of hours to prepare. I'll have to do it this time, I can't possibly bother Helen Davis again."

"Right, ok I'll go ask Jacko to do the business and send Dusty round to Johnson's house. If he won't co-operate perhaps his wife will. She was pretty pissed off as I remember and could prove useful. Give you time to prepare a statement for the vultures waiting to pick our bones clean. I'll get them to call on Cora, they could well get one positive ID on Mitchell."

"Not just any old gem, a real diamond," he said, giving her the thumbs up.

"Yeah, well as I said appraisal report should be glowing."

He looked up at her, smiled and ushered out of the room with a dismissive wave.

"I'm going, I'm going," she said, closing his office door firmly behind her and nearly running into Helen Davis.

"Sorry Ma'am, didn't see you there," Mo said apologetically.

"No worries DI Connolly, is he in?"

"Yes Ma'am and he'll be more than pleased you're here."

"Press Office phoned me about an hour ago. They knew I had some involvement, they couldn't get hold of Jake but they needed to arrange something sharpish. I was in Oxford so I drove over to see if I could be of help."

"I'm sure DCI Summers will welcome it," Mo said, stepping aside so Helen Davis could gain access to Jake's office.

"Or tell me to mind my own business."

"Never do that. Good to see you Ma'am, thought I heard your voice, come on in," Jake said, opening his door and beaming at Helen Davis.

Mo glanced at Jake and saw the delight on his face.

"Nice to see you again Ma'am," and moved away towards Jacko's desk.

"You too Mo," Helen Davis said as she went into Jake's office. As she closed the door behind her Mo heard her say "so Jake, tell me what's our latest press release gonna be?"

She went over to Jacko, asked him to find out what he could about Johnson's relatives and then asked Miller and Grey to quiz Marilyn Johnson too.

Hearing her phone ringing Mo returned to her office. It was Freddie Saunders.

"Couldn't get hold of Jake, his calls are on hold but I thought you'd like to know that I'll be doing Vicky Bennett's PM in the morning. I've had a preliminary look and like the others she was strangled and had the thrupenny piece stitched into her vagina. So same MO but he went a step further this time and stitched one into her mouth too. The killer must be a numismatist, he seems to have an unending supply of thrupenny bits. What'd make of it?"

She told him Gregg's theory and that Jaime Summers had backed it up.

"Interesting!" but Mo knew he'd lost interest when in the next breath he spewed out "gotta go, bodies waiting, just wanted to let you know about Vicky Bennett, tell Jake. Will you be attending tomorrow?"

"Someone will Freddie, but I think I've had my fix of formaldehyde for the foreseeable future."

She heard him chortling.

"You may laugh Freddie but my lungs are in need of recovery time. Seriously, thanks for letting us know." She could still here him laughing as she put down the phone and thought 'odd has to be a pre-required trait for becoming a pathologist'.

The day didn't improve. Jacko came back with a negative result.

"Clive Johnson was born in the Newbury district in the June quarter of 1977. His mother's name was Tysoe. There are no other births listed for Johnson and Tysoe so my guess is he was an only child."

Miller's news was no better. "Marilyn Johnson told us that Clive doesn't have any brothers or sisters. Her actual words were "when they saw him pop out they couldn't risk having another one". Clive hasn't returned to the family home and Marilyn Johnson said he's probably holed up with his old man in Thatcham. Apparently his mother's dead but his father still lives in Thatcham. Want us to check?"

Mo couldn't see the point, two different sources both giving the same answer, why waste more time on it?

"We did get a positive ID from Cora, but you were expecting that anyway weren't you Guv?" Miller said.

"Yeah, just confirms our latest theory."

He looked at her quizzically.

"Two Mitchells out there and we lifted the wrong one."

The press conference was just the perfect end to the perfect day. Fortunately, Helen Davis was the perfect person to keep the newshounds at bay. She just gave the statement that she and Jake had prepared saying basically "the body of another woman was found earlier today at an address in Newbury and her death was probably linked to the other murders. The police took a man into custody late last night but he was released earlier today without charge."

She ignored further questions and comments such as 'can we assume there's a serial killer on the loose?', 'The police have made no headway in finding the person responsible', 'Can we expect an early arrest?'

Unable or unwilling to answer, Helen Davis brought the press conference to a swift conclusion. The reporters left feeling cheated and looking visibly disappointed. "Their problem, not ours. Doubtless they'll come up with some sensationalised aspect of the case to accompany their by-lines," was the parting quip by Helen Davis as she left.

"Sod of a day Mo, a lot's happened but we've been stymied at every turn. We're still left asking who the hell David Mitchell is?"

"Let it go Jake, tomorrow's another day." Deep down she felt as frustrated as he did and both left the building in sombre mood.

45

I walk into the house, call out "I'm home" and almost feel depressed cos there's no one home to hear me. I go into the kitchen, grab a beer from the fridge, remove the cap and take a long swig from the bottle and then the gratitude kicks in. No nagging voice telling me not to drink from the bottle, in fact thinking back I was barely allowed to breathe. Instead of depressed I feel elated, able to do exactly as I please, when I please. So tonight I'll order Chinese takeaway, drink beer and slob out in front of the TV. I pick up the phone order a number 7 and 23 from the Jade Palace menu and eagerly await my delivery of egg fried rice and chicken with green peppers in a black bean sauce. I wander into the lounge, take another long swig of beer, relax into my comfy armchair and, glancing at my watch, realise it's almost time to catch the local news.

'A thirty seven year old man was taken into custody late last night in connection with the recent West Berkshire killings of Zak and Zoe Dryden and Natalya Birinov. Both women worked as hostesses at the Blue Lagoon Club in Newbury'

The headliner from the newscaster has certainly captured my attention and I listen attentively as the main report is broadcast.

'Clive Johnson, a 37-year-old businessman, was arrested late last night in connection with three murders in the West Berkshire town of Newbury. He was released earlier today without charge. At a press conference given by Thames Valley police late this afternoon, it was revealed that another body had been discovered at a canal-side property here in Newbury. The body was identified as 25-year-old sex worker Victoria Bennett. The body was discovered by the victim's flatmate when she returned home from a night spent in Reading. Police suspect the person responsible for Victoria Bennett's death is also the person they

are looking for in connection with the other deaths. Assistant Chief Constable Helen Davis was reluctant to comment further, other than to reiterate that the investigation was in the capable hands of DCI Jake Summers and his team of detectives and that she was confident of a positive outcome. Gina Giles Newbury.'

No longer relaxed I switch off the TV. My first reaction is anger. I hadn't expected Roxy's body to be found so quickly. Cow told me her flatmate was away for a week . I can't believe she was only 25, the hag looked nearer forty but I admit her fit body made up for her careworn features.

Anger is replaced with panic. They actually had Clive in custody that means they know he was doubling as David Mitchell. They'll recognise him as Mitchell at the club but Kate Davis only knows me as Mitchell. She's my Achilles heel, the one person who can identify me as Mitchell and lead to my downfall. I can't relax tonight, I can't risk leaving my destiny to chance. Kate's gotta go and go tonight.

It's impossible to settle, my nerves are jangling, I find myself pacing again but I must show restraint, wait until darkness falls, less chance of being seen. The front doorbell ringing makes me jump, must be the takeaway. Even the smell can't tempt me, I manage a couple of mouthfuls and scrape the remainder into the bin. My stomach is empty and growling but my mind won't let me eat. I am consumed by the need to act and knowing I have hours to wait before I can. I rehearse the scenario in my mind. She lives above the business, I know because she excused herself before we started the past life regression to get two glasses of water. When she returned we discussed the benefits of living above the business. Everywhere probably shuts by 6pm on Brookland Avenue but there are lots of flats above the shops there so I'll have s to park at least one street away and walk. Can't risk my car being identified near the scene. My next concern is how do I gain access? She won't answer the door to me. This has me in turmoil for almost an hour but then I experience one of those eureka moments that clears the mist and gives the perfect answer to the problem. She has one of those intercom systems, I'll identify myself as that Summers' guy, she'll think it's the police and let me in.

I have a plan, it's dark outside, time to see it through.

46

Jake sprawled on the sofa feeling well fed but completely dissatisfied. Four murders and the killer still at large. A wave of disappointment washed over him and must have shown on his face because Jaime, curled up beside him asked, "want to talk about it?"

"You know me so well," he said, cupping her lovely face in his hands.

"When I see frown lines wrinkling that handsome brow I don't need to be a genius to know something's troubling you and Confucius he say 'a problem shared is a problem halved.'"

He laughed. "I doubt Confucius ever said that, it's an English proverb."

She punched him lightly on the arm. "Semantics. I'm a writer, I don't deal in reality. Anyway who said it is irrelevant, it holds true so tell me."

He spent the next hour telling her about the frustrations of his day.

"I just feel as if when one door opens it's immediately slammed shut in our faces. We're getting nowhere with this investigation Jaime."

"You're so wrong Jake, you're letting frustration cloud you judgement. Cora has identified Johnson as the Mitchell she knows. Kate is adamant it's not the same man that she knows as Mitchell. Forrester agrees both recognising the similarities between the two men, so you working the relative angle is a positive move."

"But ..."

"Yeah I know, Jacko can't find brothers, the Johnson woman says he has none but what about cousins Jake? Get Jacko to check out Johnson's parents. Do they have siblings? If so there could be a few male cousins knocking around."

"I love discussing things with you, you have enough positive thoughts for the both of us. Your optimism's contagious. Come here gorgeous, if I did one right thing in my life it was marrying you," he said, pulling her into her arms.

She was about to suggest that they took this upstairs when the phone rang. She moved out of his arms to answer it but he pulled her back. "Let it ring."

"Can't, it could be important."

"More important than this," he said pouting.

"I'll let you know when I've answered it," she said, escaping his embrace.

"Hi Kate. No he's right here and sulking."

"Christ Kate, under no circumstances let him in. I'll get Jake to phone the station get a car round to you as soon as possible, just stay put. Whatever you do, don't open the door. Pack a bag and Jake will get his men to bring you here, at least you'll be safe. They'll identify themselves by saying Jaime Lechampstead, you got that Kate? Jaime Lechampstead."

Jake was up and standing by her side when she put the phone down.

"What the hell's happening, that sounded frantic."

"It is, there's a man at Kate's door claiming to be you. You heard what I told her to do."

He grabbed the phone. Told the duty sergeant, he thought it was Walsh, to get a patrol car round to 3 Brookland Avenue as soon as possible, to arrest anyone seen hanging around outside and then identify themselves to the owner with the passwords Jaime

Lechampstead.

"And Sergeant, get someone there quickly, the woman inside could be in grave danger. When they've secured the scene I want the woman Kate Davis, brought here okay?" He put the phone down turned to Jaime.

"Under control, a car should be there in five. It's gotta be Mitchell, thank God she had the foresight to ring before she let the bastard in. No point in driving to the station until I know what's gone down. I suspect if it's Mitchell he'll be long gone before the car gets there."

"Jake you're gabbling. I know you desperately want to be there directing operations but you're here, a good twenty minutes away, so let's wait calmly for Kate to arrive. All will be revealed and then you can make decisions."

He knew she was right, he couldn't achieve anything at the moment so he grinned boyishly. "Time for a quickie then?"

She just laughed.

47

I parked on Frodsham Street just a few hundred yards from Brookland Avenue and went the rest of the way on foot. It was a warm evening, my head was covered by the hoodie, making a couple of middle-aged passers-by give me a wide birth, probably believing I was some sort of reprobate. If only they knew. By the time I arrived outside number three I was hot and uncomfortable and anxious to get inside and remove the accursed hood. I pressed the intercom button and heard Kate Davis say yes?

"Police, DCI Summers Ms Davis, can we have a word?"

"Jake is that you?"

Shit they're on first name terms.

"Yes its Jake Kate, I need to talk to you about David Mitchell."

"Its late Jake , can't it wait 'til tomorrow? I'm just running a bath."

"Sorry Kate it's urgent. We're about to make an arrest but we need a positive ID from you first."

"Okay, fine, give me five minutes to empty the bath and get dressed and I'll buzz you in."

I'm getting impatient now. It's been more than five minutes so I buzz again. No answer, then I hear the wailing sound of a police siren. Of course there'll be no answer, the bitch has called the cops. I leg it as fast as I can, take the first turning right out of Brookland Avenue and then another left into a small side street that runs beside a builders merchants. A wire mesh fence separates the builders' yard from the street. Suddenly, out of nowhere, a bloody Alsatian appears running alongside me on the other side of the fence barking its fucking head off, creating enough noise to wake the dead. Shit, shit, shit, now what? I keep running leaving the yapping dog in my wake and then up ahead I see an alley, dart into it and discover that I'm behind a row of terraced houses. I have no idea where I am only that I've been heading in the general direction of Frodsham Street. I'm still running and the bloody dog is still barking. I reach the end of the alley and am heartily relieved to find that it opens out into Frodsham Street and I can see my car parked a few yards on the left. I open the driver's door, slide behind the wheel and take a few seconds to catch my breath before driving home, completely knackered but none-the-less unscathed.

48

The phone rang, Jake answered.

"Summers," he said, and then spent the next few minutes listening to the caller at the other end.

"Thanks for ringing Joe and thanks for acting so promptly."

He rang off, Jaime looked at him quizzically. "Well?"

"That was Joe Walsh ," she raised an eyebrow," the on duty sergeant at the station."

"And?" she asked impatiently.

"Kate's safe and well and should be here within the next ten minutes."

"Did they catch him?"

"No such luck, didn't spot anyone. Heard a dog barking several streets away but nothing else. I guess the sirens frightened the bastard off."

"What is it with the police and sirens? Surely a stealthy approach is more effective, especially if your aim is to catch an offender."

"Take your point but it's a double edged sword really. No sirens and traffic isn't aware so doesn't make allowances. Sirens frightens the felon off. Depends what the priorities are, if innocent people are involved, like Kate, the priority has to be their safety and that means the police arriving at the scene as quickly as possible."

"Okay, I get that and, like you say, Kate is safe and that's wonderful news. I've been meaning to ask, was Farraday able to identify anyone fitting Mitchell's description?"

"No he wasn't. Good idea but yet another dead end I'm afraid."

Twenty minutes later Kate, Roy Cummings, Jason Dobbs, Jaime and Jake were sitting round the kitchen table drinking tea and discussing how events at Brookland Avenue had played out."

Kate suspicions were first aroused when the man introduced himself as DCI Summers and then went on to call her Ms Davis.

"Too formal, when I consider Jaime and Jess to be friends," she explained. "Furthermore, I was sure you wouldn't turn up at my door without phoning first, so I made an excuse to keep him waiting and rang here. The wisest decision I've ever made, I think. But then all the warning signs and the constant advice from Jaime and Jess to be on my guard, it seemed the obvious thing to do."

"Smart move Kate, firstly going with your gut instinct and then taking heed of sensible advice. It kept you safe and to remain safe you're welcome to stay here until we catch this guy."

"Thanks for the offer Jake but it will be easier for me to stay with Linda. She only lives a few minutes away from the business, but I'm more than grateful to accept your hospitality tonight."

"Good. Okay so Roy, Jason, Sergeant Walsh tells me the coast was clear when you arrived at Brookland Avenue."

"Yes Sir," Dobbs replied. "We got the call and decided we needed to get to the scene as quick as we could so we used the sirens. Can't take chances when a life's at risk, but it probably scared him off, sorry Sir".

"You did exactly the right thing Jason. Kate's here safe so not to worry, we can nab him another day." Jake turned his head and winked at Jaime.

Dobbs and Cummings stood. "Thanks for the cuppa Ma'am. We'd better get back on patrol, there's plenty more villains to deal with out there."

"If ever you fancy an holistic treatment, it's yours. On the house," Kate said as they were leaving.

"I don't even know what an holistic treatment is ma'am, sounds painful so I'll pass. But thanks for the offer," Dobbs said.

Jake saw them out and heard Cummings mimicking Dobbs. "I don't know what an holistic treatment is ma'am! You twat Dobbs, she was offering us a free massage."

For the first time that day Jake wanted to have a real belly laugh.

49

WEDNESDAY

Kate was awake early. Disturbed by thoughts of what might have happened if she hadn't exercised caution, she'd slept fitfully. She glanced at the bedside clock, it was almost 6am. The house was quiet so she slipped out of bed pulled a book, one of Jaime's called 'Darkness and Beyond,' from a nearby shelf. Big mistake, as she started to read she freaked. The prologue introduced a killer who preyed on lone women in their apartments. She slammed it shut and hurriedly returned it from whence it came, thinking 'idiot Jaime writes crime fiction, what did you expect Mary Poppins?' Then she heard movement, someone was obviously up and about so she went into the en-suite showered, dressed and went downstairs. She found Jaime in the kitchen wearing an oversized terry towelling bathrobe, brewing fresh coffee and munching toast covered in what looked like piccalilli. She couldn't help grimacing, 'is that what I think it is?"

"Yep, piccalilli on toast, this pregnant woman's must have breakfast. Bizarre I know but I absolutely adore it," Jaime explained, laughing at Kate's horrified expression. "Don't worry Kate, I'll be offering you a choice of conventional breakfast fare. Did you sleep well?"

"Honestly no, don't get me wrong the bed was exquisitely comfortable but I had too much on my mind. Conjuring up scenes of what could have happened to me. Ridiculous I know, I was here and safe but the mind is a law unto itself."

"Not surprised, this case has certainly given Jake a few restless nights."

"What gives Jake restless nights?" he asked, walking into the kitchen. "Morning Kate."

"This accursed case darling," Jaime replied, smiling up at her husband.

Jake was suited and booted, looking well groomed and handsome and Kate couldn't help thinking 'you're a lucky woman Jaime Summers' and then wishing there was someone special in her own life.

"Piccalilli's obviously off the menu so what would you two like for breakfast?" Jaime asked.

Jake opted for cereal, toast and coffee and Kate settled for the same.

He was ready to leave the house by 7:50am and gave Kate the option of driving in with him or going in with Jaime later.

"If you could drop me at Linda's house I'll go now. I can't face going back to the flat alone."

"No problem," Jake said.

Kate hugged Jaime. "Thanks again for last night, I really appreciate it."

"No worries and Kate, be diligent, don't take anything for granted and stay safe."

Twenty minutes later Jake dropped her off at Linda's house and waited outside in the car until she was safely inside and then drove to work.

As he drove in Mo was parking her car. He pulled into his bay got out and called her over. He spent the next few minutes relating the events of the previous evening.

"Thank God she had the sense to call you. The outcome could have been so different, we might have been dealing with another dead body today."

"Yeah, doesn't bear thinking about does it. Kate's a canny lady though, she sensed the danger and acted accordingly."

50

The squad room was buzzing. Dusty Miller and Rhona were clustered together, as were Gregg and Halliday and, as usual, Jacko was tapping away at his computer keyboard. The room quieted as in turn they spotted Jake and Mo.

"Something happened last night so we need to bring you guys up to date," Jake announced, gesturing towards the boardroom.

"We know about Kate Davis Guv," Miller interrupted. "We heard it on the grapevine, Jason Dobbs loves a drama."

"Okay Dusty but there's other things to discuss so shall we?" he said, walking into the adjoining room.

Vicky Bennett's photograph was now alongside the others on the board and as they sat down Jake pointed to it.

"We're lucky that Kate Davis's photo isn't joining the victims' gallery today. She remains at risk while this bastard still at large. He's aware, presumably from the media's fascination with all things criminal, that a suspect has been released without charge. That suspect was Clive Johnson aka David Mitchell. Johnson readily admits to using the alias and we also have a positive ID from Cora Allen. So Johnson was and admits to being one of Zoe Dryden's regular clients. But Kate Davis was adamant that Johnson was not the David Mitchell that consulted her. However, both she and Mark Forrester admitted there were similarities between the two men.

As far as we know Kate Davis remains the only one who can

positively ID the other David Mitchell. And coincidentally or not someone called at her flat last night hoping to gain access by pretending to be me. So guys, anybody got any thoughts?"

Rhona Grey raised her hand.

"I'm thinking that the guy who consulted Kate Davis knows Clive Johnson; knows he was using the alias Mitchell and because of the looks thing he could be related to Johnson. If he knew Johnson was visiting the Blue Lagoon he could have targeted Zoe Dryden because of the link. Can't put a finger on the motive though."

Dusty Miller raised a hand.

"We know Johnson doesn't have brothers or sisters. Come to that Guv, Jacko couldn't find any siblings and the wife Marilyn confirmed there were none."

"True," Jake said, "but we haven't checked cousins have we?"

"I was thinking exactly that," said Jacko. "I was already working on it before we came in here. The annoying thing is I can't find any record of a marriage between a Johnson and Tysoe. There are about 30 records of men with the surname Johnson getting married in the Newbury registration district between 1967 and 1977, the year Clive was born, but none married a Tysoe so now I'm thinking perhaps they didn't marry."

"Well not in the Newbury area anyway," Mo said.

"Not even that Guv, taking Britain as a whole there's only one record of a Tysoe marrying a Johnson and that's a Celia Johnson marrying a Neil Tysoe in Leeds in 1935. Not even the right male female combination."

Jake could see Mo's brain was working overtime. "Well how about if Tysoe was her birth name but she married someone before Johnson. She reverts to her maiden name to register Clive's birth but married Johnson under her first husband's surname?"

"Yeah, that would work, I can see I'm gonna be busy. It'd be easier if we had a Christian name for Johnson's father."

"That easily rectified, I'll ring Marilyn Johnson. Apparently Johnson senior's still alive and living in Thatcham and that's where his repulsive son has slunk to," Rhona said, quick to volunteer for the task.

"So we've come to the consensus that the Mitchell Kate Davis knows is a person of interest?"

They nodded their agreement.

"Okay, let's focus our attention on finding this guy, it's not going to be easy but it seems he's our only positive lead at the moment."

Mo followed Jake into his office and shut the door.

"If this guy's our killer, should we be offering Kate Davis some protection? She could be in real danger."

"We neither have the budget nor the evidence to warrant any I'm afraid Mo."

"So let me get this right, if she's found murdered we simply tell the world we couldn't afford to protect her?" Mo said angrily.

"Don't shoot the messenger Mo, tell the powers that be, they're the ones that control the budgets."

"Sorry Jake, I wasn't directing my anger towards you, it's just red tape, brings out the worst in me."

"I do understand, it frustrates me too. However, I'm not too worried about our Kate, she's got her head screwed on and she doesn't plan to spend time alone until he's caught. Changing tack, who gets mortuary duty today? Freddie was asking if we'd be attending."

"That's one perk of being the boss Mo, we can pick and choose. Formaldehyde is not my choice of aftershave today, you wanna go?"

"Not bloody likely, lets share it round a bit shall we?"

"Fine by me, I'll leave it to you to choose."

She left his office and looked around the room. Rhona was on the phone presumably in conversation with Marilyn Johnson, Jacko was doing Jacko type things on his PC so she zeroed in on Dusty Miller.

"Sergeant Miller, we need an attendee at the PM of Vicky Bennett which is scheduled to take place in about an hour. Do I have a volunteer?"

"Yeah, I'll go Guv," he said, knowing full well he'd be going whether or not he volunteered.

"Thanks Dusty, one volunteer's worth ten pressed men. Take your old garden gate Gregg with you," she said smiling. "I know he savours the smell of the mortuary."

"You're learning Guv, you'll be speaking fluent cockney soon."

"Heaven forbid Dusty. Go give Dave the good news."

After getting a "thanks Guv" and a dirty look from Gregg, she waited for them to leave and then asked Halliday to join her in the office.

He looked nervous. "Sit down and take that worried look off your face, I don't bite."

"Glad to hear that Ma'am, I'm not up to date with my rabies shots." Then thinking he'd gone too far he blushed and said apologetically, "sorry Ma'am just a joke."

She had to laugh, the young DC was acquiring a sense of humour and beginning to fit nicely into the department.

"Cheeky," she said, wagging an index finger at him. "So Steve, how's the Jamieson case going?"

"It isn't Ma'am, Paul Jamieson definitely has an unshakeable alibi and we're no nearer finding the car that killed her. It's been hidden so well it might never surface, or my preferred theory is it's been re-cycled by one of those scrap metal processing plants. I hate to say this, but I think this is one case that could remain unsolved."

"Steve, Steve, dismiss that thought, we don't do unsolved in this department. Did you lean on Jamieson?"

"No need to Ma'am, he was at work when she was killed. Locked in his office all afternoon involved in a video conference. In fact his secretary, Deirdre Phillips, said she could still hear voices when she left at 5:30pm so didn't even disturb him to say goodnight. So, as I said, the guy has a water tight alibi."

"But does he Steve? It's easy to fake a conference call behind closed doors. Is there another way out of Jamieson's office other than via the eagle eye of Deirdre Phillips?"

"Can't say Ma'am, we never got to see the inside of his office, he came out to meet with us. Sent Deirdre off for tea and then we sat round her desk for the duration of the meeting."

"Didn't that strike you as odd?"

"Didn't cross my mind, I found him odd so just assumed his behaviour followed suit."

"Odd, how'd mean?"

"Arrogant most of the time, but every so often I got the impression he was nervous and twitchy, just odd."

"I think I'd like to see our Mr Jamieson for myself. Where does he work?"

"He's the Managing Director of Digby Engineering in Thatcham, took over when his father-in-law Ewan Digby died a couple of years ago. The company was left to his daughter Christine, but Jamieson runs it and I guess now he owns it too."

"Well, well how convenient is that? Describe Jamieson for me Steve."

"Again strange looking guy, about 5'10"/5'11" tall, slim build, short dark hair, heavy framed specs hiding pale blue eyes. The dark hair makes his fair skin appear even paler than it is. Are his looks important Guv?"

"Not sure Steve, they could be. By the way, congratulations, you just became a fully-fledged member of Newbury CID."

"Guv?"

"Yep, you've finally learned the lingo. Ma'am has, hopefully, disappeared forever?"

He laughed. "Old habits die hard Guv, Inspector Leyland was such a stickler for protocol."

"A bit of a dinosaur our Barry, but don't tell him I said so."

Steve Halliday laughed again.

"Back to business. Follow me, I want DCI Summers to hear what you just told me," Mo said, striding towards Jake's office.

Jake listened intently while Halliday repeated the information he'd given Mo.

As soon as Halliday finished, Mo jumped in. "Thanks Steve. I'll be with you in a sec, I just want a word with DCI Summers."

Halliday returned to his desk leaving an excited Mo to ask Jake "so are you thinking what I'm thinking?"

"And that would be?" he said smiling, knowing exactly what she was thinking.

"His wife dies leaving him a wealthy businessman and the business just happens to be Digby Engineering. A massive coincidence considering that Zoe Dryden's brother-in-law, Rob Preston, also works there. Furthermore, he fits Cora Allen's description of one Bernard Matthews who was one of Zoe's regulars, need I say more?"

"You think Paul Jamieson killed his wife and is also somehow connected to the deaths of our four murder victims. Yes?"

"I don't believe in coincidences Jake and they just keep on piling up. Let's just say I want to take a closer look at Mr Jamieson."

"Definitely worth a look Mo but don't be too disappointed if they are just that, coincidences. He's not our David Mitchell is he?"

"No."

"You were convinced he was our killer until fifteen minutes ago."

"That hasn't necessarily changed, Jamieson could be involved too. But I definitely fancy him for his wife's death, if only indirectly responsible. Gut feeling."

"Then get over there and check him out."

"On my way as we speak ," she said over her shoulder as she left his office.

51

Paula the redheaded receptionist at Digby's beamed at Steve Halliday as they approached the desk. Then recognizing Mo completely ignored her by addressing Steve directly.

"DC Halliday nice to see you again, how can we help?"

Before he could answer Mo interrupted.

"We're here to see Mr Paul Jamieson."

"I'll ring through and tell him you're here."

"No need thanks Paula, we know the way we'll just go on up." Mo turned her back on the receptionist and walked over to the lift, feeling the redhead's eyes boring into the back of her head as she went.

"She doesn't like you Guv," Steve said, as the lift doors closed on them.

"We have history," Mo said, shrugging her shoulders. "I don't like her much either but she definitely has the hots for you young man."

"Too bad Guv, I don't like her much either."

They exited the lift on the second floor, turned right and Steve knocked on the first office door on the left and opened it.

The office was large and airy. A plump woman behind the mahogany desk stood as they entered.

"How nice to see you again Steven and you must be Inspector

Connolly?" she said, looking at Mo and extending a well-manicured hand.

"You have me at a disadvantage, I'm afraid," Mo said, taking the outstretched hand.

"Deidre Phillips, Mr Jamieson's 'Girl Friday'. Paula rang and said you were on your way up."

"Ah that explains everything, the efficient Paula announced our arrival," Mo said, appraising the woman in front of her. No way could Deirdre Phillips be described as anyone's 'Girl Friday'. She had to be 60+ and, despite carrying some extra pounds, was elegantly dressed in a powder blue outfit that almost matched the colour of her immaculately coiffed hair. One of the blue rinse brigade, she probably voted Tory and was a stalwart of the Women's Institute.

"No David today, Steven?"

Steve shook his head. "Busy elsewhere I'm afraid."

"Shame, such an amusing fellow with his Cockney accent and that rhyming slang he uses. You're very lucky to have two such nice, young men working for you Inspector."

"I am?" Mo said, quizzically raising her eyebrows. Then seeing Deidre's crestfallen expression said "just joking Mrs Phillips, they're two of the good guys."

"Deidre, please."

"Well Deidre, I don't want to appear rude but we do need to get on. Could you tell Mr Jamieson we're here?"

"Of course," she said, picking up the phone.

As she did, the inner office door opened and Mo got her first glimpse of Paul Jamieson, and she had to agree with Halliday, he was indeed an odd looking man. With his dark hair, pale complexion and those heavy rimmed glasses he looked more like a middle-aged Goth than a businessman.

"Inspector Connolly and DC Halliday Mr Jamieson, could we have a word?"

He came out of his office closing the door behind him. "You have news about Christine?"

"Shall we take this into your office sir?"

"No need, Deidre knows everything about the case, you can speak freely in front of her. So have you arrested anyone?"

"Sorry we haven't and we're actually here to discuss another matter."

"Another matter, my beloved Christine's been killed and you're her to discuss another matter. What can be so important that it takes a senior officer away from finding my wife's killer and to come here to discuss something that can only be trivial in comparison?"

"Let me explain," Mo said calmly. "We have reason to believe you're acquainted with Zoe Dryden, as is another friend, a Mr Bernard Matthews. Is that correct sir?"

Paul Jamieson, suddenly looking extremely furtive, opened his office door. "You'd better come in."

They followed him into the spacious inner office. Situated on the back wall, in front of another door, was a bow fronted walnut desk which Jamieson walked over to and sat behind and then indicated that they should pull up chairs opposite him.

"So Mr Jamieson, we can safely assume that you are known as Bernard Matthews at the Blue Lagoon Club on Fenton Street and that in that guise you were a regular client of Zoe Dryden, a woman found murdered in her own home just a few days ago."

"I hope you're not suggesting I had anything to do with that."

"I'm not suggesting anything Paul, I'm trying to establish the facts. So did you know Zoe Dryden?"

"Yeah I knew her."

"Did you visit her at the Blue Lagoon Club and pay her for sex on a regular basis?"

"Yes."

"Were you known as Bernard Matthews when you visited the club?"

"Yes."

"Why?"

"Why what?"

"Why did you call yourself Bernard Matthews?"

"Surely that's obvious, I didn't want my bloody wife to find out."

"Suddenly she's you bloody wife Paul, just a few minutes ago she was your beloved Christine."

Obviously rattled by the questions, Jamieson began to look increasingly uncomfortable under Mo's constant scrutiny. Suddenly he was anxious to explain the outburst and decided honesty was the best policy.

"You must understand Inspector that although I loved my wife we did have problems in the bedroom department. She was no longer interested in the physical side of our marriage so I simply went elsewhere. I didn't want her to find out so I used another name, nothing more sinister than that. I liked Zoe, I would never harm her."

Although unconvinced by his change from arrogant prick to contrite husband, Mo could do little else but to say "well thanks for being so frank Paul, I think that's all for now, we'll be in touch. Out of interest, the door behind you, where's it go to?"

"Nowhere, it's a bathroom. See for yourself," he said, standing and opening the door inwards. "Exclusive use, perk of the job."

Mo could see a loo opposite the door, a wash basin beside it and what appeared to be a shower cubicle on the right hand side. Above the loo a frosted window had a small opening that a two-year-old would have difficulty clambering through. So the only way out of here was via the outer office and Deirdre Phillips.

As they left the building Mo turned and waved to Paula and was rewarded with an icy glare.

A worried Deirdre Phillips waited until the detectives left before asking her boss about Zoe Dryden.

"Wasn't she the woman that was murdered Paul? Did you know her? Who is Bernard Matthews?"

Question after question spewed out of her mouth. Jamieson just stood there patiently until she finished.

"Calm down Deirdre, there's nothing to worry about. It was a case of mistaken identity, some guy called Matthews apparently bears a striking resemblance to me. He's the man they need to question, not me. As soon as I put them straight they went away happy. So cheer up, it's nothing more than a storm in a teacup."

Placated and reassured that her boss wasn't some sort of maniacal monster she smiled up at him and returned to her desk.

52

As they drove away from Digbys Mo was anxious to hear Steve Halliday's take on the meeting with Jamieson.

"Your impression Steve?"

"Simple Guv, he's a slippery bastard with an answer for everything. Don't believe the beloved wife bit, basically I don't like him and I don't trust him but the fact remains he was locked into a video conference when Christine was killed. No way to leave the building without Deirdre seeing him. He could be involved in his wife's death but he didn't kill her, did he? "

"I think he did, I don't know how he did but my gut instinct rarely lets me down. What about Zoe and the others? Could he be involved in their deaths?"

"Hard to say Guv, he readily admitted using the name Matthews and visiting the club but then I guess he knew it was pointless to deny it when Cora Allen could so easily identify him. In my view he definitely warrants a closer look."

"My thoughts exactly."

They drove the rest of the way in companionable silence.

Just before Mo arrived back at the station, Jacko popped his head round Jake's door.

"Got a minute, Guv?"

"Only if you're the bearer of good news," Jake joked.

"Oh, I think you'll like this Guv. Snippet of information that might change the course of this inquiry, interested?"

"Very, and I think DI Connolly will be too," he said, spotting Mo arriving back at base. "Let's take this next door, there's more room to spread out."

Jake followed Jacko out of the office and beckoned Mo over to join them in the boardroom.

"Jacko has news," he said, as they say down. Thought you might like to hear it too. So Jacko, what've you got for us?"

"Well it all stems from Inspector Connolly's suggestion that maybe Tysoe had been married before and guess what? She was spot on. Rebecca Tysoe married a Carter Jamieson in Reading in September 1970 and their son Paul Jamieson was born there in July1972. Rhona supplied Johnson's Christian name. It was Drew, so although Johnson's as common as muck Drew isn't, so that made things much easier. I was able to find a marriage between a Drew Johnson and Rebecca Jamieson in Newbury in March 1976 and their son Clive was born in July 1977. So Paul Jamieson and Clive Johnson are half-brothers. Now that's what I call interesting."

Mo leapt up and planted a kiss on Jacko's cheek. "I could kiss you John Jackson."

"I think you just did Guv."

"I'm tempted to kiss you myself," Jake said.

"You're alright Guv, I'll settle for DI Connolly's thanks."

Jake laughed. "Well, you've certainly given us food for thought and I think it's time to share it with the team and reassess. I just caught a whiff of formaldehyde so I guess that means that DS Miller and Dave Gregg are back on board."

"You definitely have a detective's nose Guv, I'll get 'em in," Mo volunteered, obviously pumped by Jacko's news.

Minutes later Jacko was repeating his discoveries to the assembled detectives.

"Thank you Jacko, you've done a great job," Jake said, after he'd finished. "Before we discuss it further let's play catch up. So Mo, tell us what happened at Digbys with Mr Paul Jamieson."

She was delighted to tell them about Jamieson, how he'd admitted to being Bernard Matthews and his association with Zoe Dryden and her gut feeling that although he had what appeared to be a cast iron alibi, he was somehow responsible for his wife's death. Then she added, "and hearing what I've just heard from Jacko, I'm even more suspicious about his involvement in the recent spate of killings."

Next up were Miller and Gregg who had little to report really other than cause of Vicky Bennett's death was confirmed as strangulation and the presence of the thrupenny pieces in her mouth and vagina were a clear indication that she was another victim of the same thruppeny piece killer, as he'd been nicknamed.

"Okay, let's have your thoughts," Jake said. "Mo, you start."

"Well, I think you're all aware that I don't believe in coincidences, never have. So the thing that strikes me most is the fact that Carter Jamieson married Rebecca Tysoe. Carter Jamieson, Jeb Carter there has to be a connection there. Add to the mix, our elusive David Mitchell who in a past life regression claimed to be Jeb Carter, a murder suspect from the 19th Century. I can't put a finger on it but there must be a link. Finding out that Johnson and Jamieson are half-brothers also begs the question, are they working in tandem? You're probably thinking that operating in tandem is rare for serial killers but we all know it does happen."

"Rhona?" Jake said, seeing her hand shoot up in the air.

"I understand where you're going with that theory Guv, but we need proof that they know of each other's existence. Johnson's wife was adamant that he had no siblings, surely she would know of Jamieson's existence if he were in contact with her husband."

"I take your point Rhona, we certainly do need to establish a link if indeed there is one."

"I think it would be good to hear what Drew Johnson has to say, we know he's still alive cos Clive's camping out at his house right now. Being married to Paul's mother means he probably knows about any fraternal relationship between the two men," Dusty interjected.

"Then that's your mission this afternoon. Go see Drew Johnson and Dusty, take a shower before you go. He's an old man, he doesn't need to be overwhelmed by the smell of formaldehyde," Jake said, causing a ripple of laughter in the room.

"Steve?" Jake said, seeing the young man was eager to speak.

"We have two cases that seem to overlap here Guv. The death of Christine Jamieson and the murders of Newbury working girls, so would it be prudent to speak with Christine Jamieson's mother? She, more than anyone, should know the true state of her daughter's marriage."

"Yeah and it would be a good idea to find out if either Jamieson or Johnson are coin collectors," Gregg added.

"All valid points," Jake said. "So Dusty, Dave go and talk to Drew Johnson. Rhona and Steve you take Mrs Digby and Jacko, try and establish a link between Carter Jamieson and Jeb Carter. We need concrete evidence before we take anyone into custody this time, so I trust you guys to get out there and do the business."

53

Left alone in the boardroom Mo and Jake had been reviewing the recent information for the past 40-minutes, both were still bothered by Mitchell. It had to be more than a coincidence that he looked like Clive Johnson, had the past life regression connection to Jeb Carter and was thought to be the last person to see Natalya Birinov alive.

"I just don't get it. We've covered just about every angle and I still can't work out how Mitchell fits in."

Jake was in complete sympathy with her growing frustration. "I'm baffled too, but every instinct tells me we're close to solving this case and then, hopefully, all will become clear."

"I hope you're right cos I can't see this bugger stopping unless he's caught and enough people have died already, including an innocent young boy."

As if by magic, Jacko appeared at that precise moment waving a sheet of paper. "Be prepared to be astounded."

"Then astound us," Mo said, making space for Jacko to sit between them.

"I knew if Jeb Carter had fathered any children it had to be with the girl who was sharing his home at the time he was killed, one Grace Chandler. Carter died in 1887 so I searched for Grace Chandler in the 1891 census and couldn't find her. Thinking she'd probably married I turned my attention to finding a husband and sure enough she'd married a Benjamin Raines in 1889. Finding the Raines family in the census was an easy task," he said, pointing to the printout in front of him. "Benjamin Raines, his wife Grace and their children Maggie Carter Raines aged 3 and Benjamin Raines aged 1. The child Grace was born two years before Grace Chandler married Raines, she also carried the name Carter so the obvious conclusion is she was Jeb Carter's daughter. In the 1901 Census she's just listed as Maggie Raines, the Carter's been dropped probably because of the notoriety surrounding the name in a small community like Stanton."

Mo visibly excited by the information punched him lightly on the arm. "Brilliant, well done Jacko."

"There's more Guv. Maggie Raines married in 1912 at the age of 24. Her husband's name was George Jamieson and their son Carter Jamieson was born in 1913. He married a Mary Jane Harrison in1943 and then in 1945 their son Carter was born, the father of Paul Carter Jamieson born 1972. So to summarise, Paul Carter Jamieson is the great, great, grandson of Jeb Carter."

"You're a diamond Jacko," Jake said, showing his enthusiasm by energetically clapping his colleague on the back.

Mo gave him a hug and planted yet another kiss on his cheek and whispered "John Jackson, you could use a shave."

Jacko blushed and rubbed the stubble on his cheeks.

"I'm amazed you found that information so quickly. I didn't realise the police had the software to access census records."

"They don't Guv, but I do. I've been researching my family history for a few years now."

"Then we're extremely grateful for your genealogy expertise."

"We're still no nearer to finding David Mitchell who, until now, was our prime suspect and the only connection we had to Jeb Carter. If we just had the name then I would be tempted to think that Jamieson was Mitchell, but we have a description and Jamieson certainly doesn't fit that, does he?"

"We need to think outside the box Mo. He doesn't look like Mitchell unless?"

"He ditches the glasses and dark hair. He has the fair complexion and blue eyes. You're thinking he was using a disguise. Why the hell didn't I think of that?"

"Don't beat yourself up. It didn't occur to me until Jacko spelled out the family history. After all, it's only a theory. We need proof before we can move on it."

"If Jamieson is Mitchell, and Mitchell is our killer, then it goes to prove what I've always believed. That some people are just born evil, it's in his genes."

"Jaime would definitely argue that point with you and I tend to agree with her. Environment is just as important, if not more so, it can and does override nature."

"Not that old chestnut, the great nurture versus nature debate."

"No, more the nature plus nurture effect. In fact scientists in America have discovered a genotype associated with psychopaths. One neuroscientist found that he had the DNA and brain patterns that could cause trouble, but he wasn't the victim of abuse or violence in childhood. The trauma trigger for initiating violence in him was missing."

"Our resident psychologist has certainly coloured your view," Mo laughed. "Don't you agree Jacko?"

Getting no answer she turned to look at him but Jacko, not interested in getting involved in a genetics debate, was long gone.

54

I smile as I watch my darling child playing in the hearth. When I look at my little Maggie, with her tousled blonde hair and blue eyes, so like the father that sired her, my heart is filled with happiness. She is the one good legacy left to me by the infamous Jeb Carter.

I couldn't believe that Jeb, the man I trusted and adored, was responsible for the death of his wife Ginny, the school master Frederick Simmons and the other two women that poor Henry King wrongfully took the blame for. When I think back to the time I spent with Jeb I realise I was so in awe of him I didn't notice his cruel streak, the vicious slaps along with the rough unloving sex he subjected me to. He never loved me, he said as much on the day he died. I don't believe he loved his wife either; the only person Jeb Carter ever loved was Jeb Carter. Now my undying gratitude has to go to Mr Monkman who I'm convinced saved me from the same fate that those other hapless women suffered. In fact, many of the villagers agree the poor man was one of Jeb Carters victims too.

It took a while before I could trust another man but then I met Benjamin Raines. His kind and caring nature persuaded me that there were still good men out there. He too had suffered at Jeb Carter's ruthless hands. His young fiancée, Esme Hawkins, was the last of Jeb's victims. Benjamin's a fine man; no he doesn't set my heart aflutter like Jeb did, but he's my husband and I've grown to love him. I know I can trust him with my life; he will never raise his hand in anger, use or abuse me or mine. From the moment we married he thought of Maggie as his own, never once mentioning that she is the daughter of a man he despises.

I glance up and see the love in my husband's eyes as he, too, watches his children at play. Maggie is hugging her younger brother, little Ben, who with his dark curls and chocolate brown eyes is so like the man who watches over him. When Ben was born my husband legally adopted Maggie; she is no longer Maggie Carter Raines just our daughter Maggie Raines. Benjamin catches my eye and winks and I smile back at my husband knowing I am truly blessed.

55

Dusty Miller didn't really know what to expect when he rang Drew Johnson's doorbell but it certainly wasn't the dignified well-dressed man that answered it. Johnson was a tall man in his mid -70s, sporting a well clipped-military style moustache and a full head of thick white hair. Clear deep set blue eyes dominated his still handsome face. Dressed in grey chinos and a grey cashmere sweater, he could almost be a septuagenarian model for GQ magazine. In fact, Miller was beginning to think they had the wrong house because he couldn't quite believe that the man standing in front of him was actually Clive Johnson's father. Nothing about him vaguely resembled the pale skinned, sandy haired Clive.

"Mr Johnson?"

"Yes."

"Police, DS Miller and DC Greg," Dusty said, showing his warrant card.

"Clive's at work."

"Actually, sir, it's you we'd like to speak with. May we come in?"

Johnson stood back from the door allowing them to enter and then ushered them into the first room on the right of the hallway. The walls were lined with bookcases filled with leather bound volumes and the room was dominated by a highly polishes mahogany antique desk covered by a green skiver embossed with fine gold tooling. The house was almost modest in comparison to its opulent furnishings.

Miller expected Johnson to sit at the desk; instead he pointed to a small circular table on the left and suggested they join him there.

"So how can I help?" Johnson asked.

"Clive's mother, your wife Rebecca, I presume you knew that she'd been married before and had a son, Paul Jamieson, from her first marriage."

"Of course, we had no secrets."

"Then can I also assume your son Clive knows he has a half-brother living locally."

"Paul lives locally? I had no idea. But your assumption that Clive knows him couldn't be further from the truth."

Dusty looked at Dave Gregg and raised his eyebrows. Johnson noticed.

"Let me be honest here, I recued my wife from an abusive marriage to Carter Jamieson and Clive doesn't even know about that. The first time I met Rebecca in 1973 she was a temporary resident at the newly opened Women's Centre in Reading for victims of domestic violence. I was the attending GP at the centre and Rebecca arrived there with a broken jaw, a fractured right arm and multiple contusions to the head and body. She was a real mess. She'd given birth to her son Paul some 6-months earlier and since his birth Jamieson had been increasingly violent, culminating in the severe beating that brought her to the centre. She told us that it was almost as if she'd become superfluous in the marriage, he had the son he so desperately wanted but he no longer wanted her. After the beating he actually told her to get out and never come back and if she ever tried to contact their son again he would kill her."

"So Paul was left with his father?"

"He was, not from choice but from necessity. It wasn't an easy decision for her but you must be aware, she was in fear for her life. She also knew Jamieson would never hurt his son so yes, she left him and regretted it every day for the rest of her life. We never told Clive because again she was afraid that if he knew then he too could be at risk from Jamieson. I resigned as a GP, we moved to Newbury and I started my own business in medical supplies. We married in 1976 and Clive was born a year later."

"So your wife never contacted her son Paul again."

"Not strictly true. After we were married, and unbeknown to me, she went to Reading thinking that maybe, because she'd stayed away for so long and was married to someone else, Jamieson would allow her contact with Paul. When she arrived Carter was a real gentleman, invited her in and made tea but the minute she mentioned wanting to see Paul he went berserk and brutally raped her."

"I trust she reported it."

"No amount of persuasion would make her, but she never ever went back there again."

"I'm sorry to ask this sir, but is Clive Johnson your son?"

"Of course he's my son. I may not be his biological father, that bastard Jamieson has that honour, but he's mine in every other way. Now you have the whole truth and the real reason that Rebecca kept her distance. She couldn't risk Jamieson finding out that he had another son who, like Paul, was the image of his father. I'd be grateful if Clive is left in ignorance, he has no idea about any of this."

"We really appreciate your candour sir and we will do our best, but I'm afraid I can't promise anything."

"One other thing," said Gregg, determined not to be left out. "Before we leave sir, does Clive happen to collect coins?"

"Not that I'm aware of but you'll need to ask him?"

"Well, thanks again for your help," Dusty said, offering his hand to Johnson as they stood ready to leave.

"Well that's a real turn up for the books Sarge," Gregg said, as soon as the front door closed behind them.

"Yeah, I think like us the Guv will be amazed by that snippet of information."

56

Steve Halliday pulled onto the gravel driveway of a 'chocolate box' detached thatched cottage in the village of Hampton Norreys. Rhona got out of the car and gazed admiringly at the 18th century country cottage in front of her.

"Isn't it magnificent Steve? Just the sort of house I'd like to own and nest in."

"I suppose, if you like that sort of thing. Personally, I prefer new builds with their clean lines and level floors. Pokey corners and low ceilings don't do it for me."

"Philistine," Rhona said, ringing the bell.

It was answered by a middle-aged, round faced, woman with twinkling blue eyes and a hairstyle that would've befitted a shaggy Old English Sheep Dog. Rhona immediately thought 'this woman's far too young to be Betty Digby'.

"DC Grey and DC Halliday here to see Mrs Digby," she said, showing her warrant card.

"Come in, she's expecting you. I'm Ursula Andrews, friend, housekeeper, constant companion and a much cheaper option than the traditional Care Home," she said, in a soft Irish brogue and then chuckled at her own joke.

The house had obviously undergone major refurbishment, the exterior belied its spacious high-ceilinged interior. At the far end of the central hallway, stairs led up to the second floor. There were two rooms leading off to the right and two to the left. Ursula directed them into the first on the left.

"It's the police Betty," she announced, in a voice louder by several decibels and then turning to Rhona whispered "she's a little deaf."

"I'm not deaf and well you know it. I just have terrible trouble understanding that County Cork accent of yours." And then laughing and addressing the detectives, "please forgive the hired help."

"I'll leave you to it then," Ursula said, turning to leave.

"She'll listen at the door, more like."

Pretending she hadn't heard, Ursula left the room as Betty Digby explained it was just light-hearted banter and that Ursula was her saviour, providing humour and care in equal measure.

The sitting room they'd entered was a large square dual aspect room with patio doors leading out to a beautifully landscaped garden. Rhona was glad to see that the room, although modernised, had retained some of its original features with its inglenook fireplace, decorative cornice and ceiling rose. Betty Digby, in her early eighties, was an elegant looking woman with fine features and soft curling grey hair. She looked completely at ease in one of the five burgundy button backed leather armchairs that matched the chaise longue and sofa that completed the seating accommodation in the room. Rhona walked over and took the old lady's hand and was surprised by the strength of her grip.

"Stunning garden you have Mrs Digby, even the added bonus of a stream running through it," said Halliday, admiring the view over the garden.

"That's no stream young man, it's the River Pang and the land you see beyond the Chinese bridge crossing it, well that's my wilderness and wild life haven."

"Wow," he said, utterly impressed.

"I don't suppose you came to discuss the merits of my garden so how can I help. Is it about Christine? Have you caught the callous cad that ran her down?"

Hearing the word cad made Rhona want to smile. "No ma'am, I'm afraid we haven't but we'd like to ask you a few questions about her husband Paul Jamieson and the state of their marriage."

Betty Digby visibly frowned at the mention of her son- in- law.

"Well I was never happy that she married him. To me he always seemed a cold fish, more interested in what the marriage could do for him than any love for Christine. Honestly though, love her as I did, sometimes I actually felt sorry for him. She was very bossy and always overly concerned about appearances. As soon as he began losing his hair she made him wear that awful black wig and then those hideous glasses, neither of which suited him. She made him into some ridiculous parody of the father she adored. He put up with it because at the end of the day he knew that Digby Engineering would be hers and by association his and now look, he has it all."

"Yes and if I believed he had the balls to kill her he'd definitely be my number one suspect."

"You were listening then?" Betty Digby said, as Ursula came back into the room carrying a tray laden with tea and biscuits.

"Too right and for what it's worth, I've never quite believed the victim persona Jamieson portrays. He's a creepy little bastard at best. Extremely rude with a condescending attitude towards me, who he considers to be less than something the dog dragged in."

"Thank you Ursula!"

"Sorry for the outburst Betty, but I just had to have my say. You'd never say it so I had to. Now can I offer you two young people tea?" she asked, placing the tray on the coffee table in front of them.

"Well as you've gone to so much trouble it would be rude to refuse wouldn't it?" Halliday said, eyeing the plate of chocolate Hobnobs.

"Have one," Ursula laughed, "they're my favourites too."

"One more thing Mrs Digby, does Paul collect coins?" Steve asked, before taking one of the proffered biscuits.

"Christine never mentioned it but I honestly don't know. Why?"

"Unusual ones have turned up in cases we're currently investigating."

"And how would that involve Paul?"

Noticing that Steve suddenly looked like a deer trapped in the beam of headlights, Rhona was quick to respond.

"It doesn't necessarily, it's just that his secretary mentioned that he collected."

"Then she knows more about him than I do," she said dismissively and Steve looked grateful to be rescued from any other searching questions.

Twenty minutes later they offered their thanks, said their goodbyes and left.

"Aren't you absolutely gobsmacked by those revelations?" Steve asked, as they drove back.

"Yeah, I'm thinking that our Mr Jamieson could look a lot more like Clive Johnson if he discarded the hair and glasses."

"Not only that, I'm thinking he knows a lot more about his wife's death than we give him credit for. Ursula was certainly a character assassin wasn't she?"

"But spot on I guess and I just love the way the two women interact. It was really refreshing to experience that sort of carer caring relationship."

"With humour added. Ursula certainly does her best to put some cheer back into the old lady's life."

"Steve Halliday, showing empathy, not such a philistine after all."

***

When they arrived back, anxious to disclose their newfound information, they bypassed Dusty and Dave in animated conversation at Jacko's desk and headed straight for Jake's office.

"They're out," Dusty shouted after them.

Rhona turned towards him, disappointment written all over her face.

"You look how we feel," Dusty said, as his two colleagues walked towards him. "Important information and no one to tell. They're at the West Berks Crem attending Natalya's funeral."

"I'd forgotten it was today."

"Same here, but the service was scheduled for 2pm so they'll be back anytime soon."

Rhona glanced up at the clock, it was it was 3:15pm.

"Well we're here, you need to talk so let's exchange info," Dusty said, in an attempt to quell Rhona's obvious disappointment.

57

The funeral was a sorry affair. If Jake and Mo were expecting the killer to put in an appearance they were sadly disappointed. Other than themselves there were only three people present, Cora Allen and Nick and Scarlet Danvers. Andrei Birinov hadn't even bothered to show at his own sister's funeral. Cora told them afterwards that the unfeeling bastard had emailed Dobson Funeral Directors with instructions, paid the bill by banker's draught and stayed well away.

"She was his sister for God sakes!" Cora said to Mo.

"Perhaps the whole thing was too painful for him."

"He was ashamed, the bastard was too ashamed to acknowledge his own sister."

"Then that's his problem and he'll have to live with it," Mo said, putting her arm around a tearful Cora.

They arrived back at the station at 3.30pm. Finding the squad room abuzz with noise and suppressed excitement, Jake walked straight through into the 'boardroom', sat down and watched as his team filed in behind him as he knew they would.

"You'd have to be senseless not to feel the highly charged atmosphere present next door, so I'm guessing you guys have news," Jake said, as soon as they'd gathered round the table.

The resulting cacophony was deafening, everyone speaking at once each trying to be the first to impart, what was to them, the most important information gleaned to date.

"Whoa, one at a time please, Dusty?"

Jake and Mo listened intently, their excitement growing with each new revelation.

When everyone had spoken Jake move over to a white board.

"So in summary," he said as he began to list the relevant points on the board in front of him, speaking and writing them down at the same time.

1.   Clive and Paul are full brothers.

2.   Clive is ignorant of Paul's existence or so Drew Johnson tells us, impossible to say if the reverse is also true.

3.   Paul wears a wig and heavy rimmed glasses disguising any likeness to Clive.

4.   Clive admits to being known as David Mitchell at the Blue Lagoon club but was not identified as such by Kate Davis. Paul also admits going to the club and using the name Bernard Matthews whilst there.

5.   Paul Jamieson has inherited Digby Engineering due to his wife's tragic, untimely demise.

"So those are the facts to date, any thoughts?" he said, returning to the table.

Mo's arm was the first to shoot into the air.

"Mo?"

"To me it's obvious Guv, Jamieson knows that Johnson exists. Whether he's known for a long time or whether he found out when they both visited the club is irrelevant, I'm convinced he knows. Therefore he's probably also aware that Johnson passed himself off as David Mitchell. So I think as well as being Cora's Mr Matthews he also visited Kate Davis in the guise of Mitchell. I think he's our David Mitchell and our killer. I also believe he is somehow involved in his wife's death. I'm undecided as to Johnson's role in all of this, if indeed he has any."

"Well Inspector Connolly clearly has Jamieson tried and convicted and, I have to say, I tend to agree with her view. Anyone think otherwise?"

The room remained silent.

"Not a peep, then I suggest we get Jamieson in, remove the wig and glasses and see if Kate Davis can do the business of identifying him. We'll need to search his house, there's more than enough evidence here to get a warrant so I'll get Inspector Long onto that. Mo, take Steve and Dave get over to Digbys' and bring Jamieson in. Dusty, you and Rhona locate Clive Johnson and invite him to come and talk to us. Go through Drew Johnson, he might have more success persuading his son to help us with our inquiries. Jacko, I'd be grateful if you could do printouts of everything connecting Jeb Carter to Jamieson, in fact everything you've discovered about both Jamieson and Johnson's complex families. I'll be spending the next hour sharing our good news with ACC Davis. Who knows, we may well have this sewn up by close of play today. It's Zoe and Zak Dryden's funeral tomorrow, now wouldn't it be fitting to tell the family we have the person responsible for their deaths in custody?"

58

I feel I'm losing my grip on reality. I hear my father's voice whispering in my ear, insistent, repeating the dreadful things he told me as a child. Describing in graphic detail the abuse he suffered at the hands of his drunken father and how it made him so determined to protect me at all costs, sheltering me from outside influence, isolating me from the natural world. Forever telling me stories of my mother's callous abandonment, her marriage to another man, a brother who receives the love and attention that should be mine. How me and my murderous ancestor Jeb Carter are bound together by an inextricable fate. Over and over until I have no alternative but to shout "shut up, shut up for God's sake shut up." I collapse into my chair in an almost fugue like state, unsure if I am myself or my nemesis Jeb Carter, seeking his revenge and retribution.

Suddenly I'm aware of Deirdre standing by the desk saying she heard me shout and asking if I'm okay. I want to tell her to bugger off instead I say "sorry Deirdre, nodded off bad dream. Not getting the sleep I should, all this worry about Christine, you know. I'll be fine thank you."

Within minutes of her leaving the office it starts again. I cover my ears hoping to block out the sound but his voice is somehow inside my head, nothing can stop it. Then it's replaced by another, the accent denoting the arrival of Jeb Carter urging me to commit despicable acts of violence in his name. I shake my head with such vigour that I feel dizzy but somehow it seems to have dislodged the demons from my brain and I can function again. For how long I cannot say. The intervals shorten between episodes and I'm sure someday soon there'll be no respite.

I feel in my bones that my days as an avenging angel, and in my more lucid moments I perceive myself as a higher being clearing the planet of its flotsam and jetsam, are drawing to a close.

The police are not idiots. Connolly already mistrusts me, they will work it out eventually and then I must make choices, fight or flight. If madness finally overtakes me then I won't know and care even less what my fate may be.

59

Mo strode up to the reception desk at Digbys. She didn't ask Paula if they could see Jamieson rather informed her that's what they were about to do. A man popped his round the door of the office behind reception.

"Inspector Connolly, I thought I recognised your voice."

"Mr Preston isn't it?"

He nodded. "Can I be of help?"

"Thanks but we're here to see Mr Jamieson."

"Fine but if you do need anything come and find me," he said, smiling but secretly wondering why the hell the police had arrived mob-handed demanding to see the boss.

Deirdre was expecting them as Mo knew she would be with the irritating Paula in charge of Reception.

"I hope you're the bearer of good news, the poor man's even dropping off to sleep at work. He's totally exhausted and undoubtedly suffering from stress," Deirdre said, as she knocked on the door of the inner office.

They waited. After about thirty seconds Deirdre knocked again, still no answer.

"He must be in the bathroom, I'll check," she said, opening the door and going in.

Mo followed her in. Deirdre knocked on the bathroom door.

"Paul are you in there?"

No answer

"He must be outside."

"Outside, how the hell did he get outside?"

"The door from the bathroom leads to the fire escape."

"Bugger, how did I miss that?"

"Easily, it's situated on the right and is obscured when this door opens inwards," Deirdre explained. "I expect we'll find him on the platform getting a breath of fresh air."

Mo pushed passed her into the bathroom and, sure enough, there was a door on the right. It was wide open and as she feared there was no sign of Paul Jamieson.

"Downstairs quick," she said to Gregg and Halliday. "The bastards getting away."

"You referring to this bastard?" Rob Preston asked, as he pushed Jamieson, minus wig and glasses, into the office in front of him.

"My God, what's happened to you Paul?" Deirdre exclaimed in horror.

Ignoring her completely Mo looked directly at Rob Preston. "Thank God, how did you know?"

"I didn't, but it struck me as odd that three police officers would turn up just to ask one man a few questions. I knew he had an escape route so I went outside and waited and, like a rat deserting a sinking ship, he scuttled out. Killed his wife did he?"

"Oh I think you'll find he's guilty of much more than that. I can't say any more now just that you'll be delighted that you stopped him in his bid for freedom."

She read Jamieson his rights, cuffed him and put him in the police car alongside Gregg, who could put the fear of God into any criminal if he was in the mood to do so. He was definitely in the mood, but it soon became obvious that the demons lurking in Jamieson's own mind were far more fearsome than anything Gregg could instill.

60

The whole team were in a jubilant mood and were enjoying a pint together in The Carpenters Arms in Donnington, which used to be Jake's local before he and Jaime moved to Leckhampstead. Jake had invited everyone involved in the case, so as well as his own people, Mike Long and his team were there as were Sergeant Walsh and PCs Dawson Dobbs and Cummings. Barry Leyland had declined the invitation as Jake knew he would. Socialising with other ranks for any reason was a definite no no in his book. Jake was sure he would have made an exception had he known that ACC Davis was putting in an appearance to offer her congratulations.

***

They had Jamieson bang to rights. Kate Davis had identified him as Mitchell and without the disguise it was easy to see the similarity between him and Johnson. Interviewed by Mo, Johnson admitted that he knew Matthews. They'd met on one occasion in the bar at the Blue Lagoon Club where Jamieson had introduced himself as Matthews and tried to engage him in conversation.

"I thought he was weird," he said, describing the meeting. "He looked strange for starters and he kept asking me personal questions about my mother. That's the only reason I remember him. It was only a brief encounter and I left as soon as politeness would allow and never saw him again."

"So Matthews, or Jamieson as we now know him, thought you were David Mitchell?"

"Everyone at the Blue Lagoon club thought I was David Mitchell, that's how I introduced myself. We've been through all of this already."

Mo disliked the man but she did believe him. He didn't know that Paul Jamieson was his brother and the inevitable realisation would doubtless horrify him. Yes he was an arse but an innocent one.

Mike Long, on searching the Jamieson house, had found irrefutable proof that he was the man responsible for his wife's death and the deaths of the other three women and Zak Dryden.

The car that killed Christine Jamieson was discovered in the garage hidden by a tarpaulin. In the house they found a recording of Jamieson's voice extolling the virtues of a product that Digbys manufactured. The same five or six sentences were recorded again and again. The disc was labelled video conference and bore the date of Christine Jamieson's murder.

In his den in a locked bureau they found cable ties of the type used to bind Natalya Birinov's wrists, duct tape, a supply of individual suture packs, a reel of nylon cord and a tin containing thrupenny pieces labelled Carter's Coin Collection. And then the clincher, a collection of trophies, photographs of the victims, each packaged in a clear polythene pocket with a personal memento, a lock of Zoe Dryden's hair, a lipstick imprint on tissue of Natalya's mouth and a cheap necklace bearing the name Roxy. No photo or memento of Zak, but then the poor kid was probably just a victim of circumstance

Yes, they certainly had him bang to rights, with that evidence there wasn't a court in the country that wouldn't convict him.

61

Dr David Lincoln, an eminent psychiatrist helping the police unravel a motive for the killings, was, in Jamieson's more lucid moments, able to establish that the past life regression experience had served to confirm to Jamieson what he already believed to be true. That indeed he was the embodiment of his ancestor James Edward Bardolf Carter. Gregg had been right about the thrupenny pieces, they were meant to signify that the women who'd died were nothing more than worthless whores. In fact, their value was less than the derogatory amount he'd stitched inside them. Stitching closed off their source of income and in Jamieson's mind ensured their purification and would prevent them from following such a profession in any subsequent lives. Lincoln said that Jamieson would never plead guilty to the murders because he truly believed that Jeb Carter killed those women and, after all, he wasn't responsible for what Jeb Carter did. In fact, David Lincoln summed it up with "I doubt he'll even get to trial, I'm sure my fellow experts will agree he's unfit to plead."

Jake ran the evidence and David Lincoln's assessment of Paul Jamieson by Jaime, who was more than qualified to give an opinion.

"From what you've told me Lincoln's probably right, and should a judge deem Jamieson fit to plead he's bound to be found guilty but insane and detained at her majesty's pleasure in a secure psychiatric unit."

"He was sane enough not to call himself Jeb Carter, to implicate the brother he'd been groomed to hate, to plan and execute killings and remove any incriminating evidence. Can a man who does all of that really be insane?"

"Insanity can be a gradual process, he shows all the symptoms of being a psychopath, feels no shame and has no remorse. Added to that, he confirms he is the re-incarnation of Jeb Carter an ancestor and a murderer. Even if you don't believe in re-incarnation you cannot deny the fact that he undoubtedly does and that, dear husband, is probably what tipped Paul Jamieson over the edge into insanity. And don't believe for one minute that people who are insane can't be manipulative, clever and devious."

"And that's me told."

"Be grateful you have enough evidence to convict whether or not he's fit to plead."

"Absolutely, no judge and jury in the land could fail to find him guilty and he will spend the rest of his life locked up one way or another."

"Result then, let it go. You've caught your killer and justice will be done ,besides we have much more pressing things to occupy our thoughts. Like have you finished your best man's speech for tomorrow's nuptials?"

"I was hoping you would lend a hand being a famous writer and all."

"I write novels not speeches."

"I promise carnal benefits."

"Then how can I refuse"

Then putting a finger to her lips said "hush now, they're coming back."

Jess had been showing her parents round the marquee that had been erected in the garden. Large enough to hold the hundred + invited wedding guests and sixty or so friends arriving for the evening celebrations and with an elegant inner lining in subtle shades of silver and blue, it was definitely fit for purpose. An L-shaped covered walkway from the patio connected the main marquee to a bar tent that would be manned by staff from the local village pub. A wooden floor had been laid in the marquee and a raised plinth at the far end housed the rectangular top table. Round tables that would seat eight occupied the remaining floor space and were already laid up with fine tableware and place names. The catering for the Wedding Breakfast was in the hands of a much recommended firm from Newbury and chefs from the Blue Lagoon were supplying the evening buffet, courtesy of Cora Allen. In fact, Cora had offered the Blue Lagoon Restaurant as a venue for the reception which was graciously declined by Mo. It was a step too far to take their guests to what was considered by some to be an upmarket Bordello, but she liked Cora and not wanting to offend accepted her offer of supplying food for the evening revellers.

As Jess explained to her parents, in the evening the top table would disappear to be replaced by a band fronted by Ray Quinn, the music teacher at her school, and the floor space would be cleared for dancing

"Well, what'd think?" Jaime asked, as they came back into the house.

"Perfect," her mother replied. "Absolutely perfect darling."

"Now how about some dinner," her father, said slipping an arm round Jaime's shoulder. "I'm famished."

Meanwhile the Connolly family were enjoying a home-cooked meal and catch up with Mo at Croft Cottage, where they were staying overnight. As always, Mo was delighted to spend time with the family she loved and missed. Her brother, Kieran, had driven down from the Midlands in the Daimler that would pick Jess up tomorrow, and her parents had come in a recently restored 1966 White Ford Mustang that Ed thought would be the perfect transport for his only much-loved daughter Maureen. He still insisted on calling her Maureen even though the rest of her family had long since slipped into the more familiar Mo.

62

The wedding was a grand affair. Conducted by a minister that looked and acted so like Geraldine Grainger that Jake was almost convinced they were in the midst of filming an episode from the 'Vicar of Dibley. As he stood waiting for Jess and Mo to arrive, he watched as her roving eye scanned the many eligible young men present finally settling on the handsome Alan Miller seated with other squad members in the third pew on the right hand side of the central aisle. Miller always dressed immaculately and with his dark haired, olive skinned Latin looks probably gave the impression of some Italian Lothario, which couldn't be further from the truth. If that's what Geraldine saw then the reality would leave her sadly disappointed. Mo's family occupied the two pews in front of her colleagues and Jake was aware of Mo's Mother fidgeting beside him, anxiously awaiting her daughter's arrival.

On the opposite side Jaime and her mother were talking together and at one point Jaime turned towards him and winked.

Her entrance heralded by 'From this Moment On' by Shania Twain and Brian Whyte, Mo was the first to arrive on the arm of Ed Connolly, every inch as handsome as his daughter was beautiful. She looked stunning in an elegant white ruffled V-neck chiffon dress with beaded waist. Her familiar spiky blonde hair had been tamed into a softer style, on the right side of her head a single peony like, white feathered flower, nestled. She stood beside Jake and he could see the happiness shining from her alluring green eyes. As the music continued to play Jess arrived. Her dress, identical to Mo's, looked equally stunning. Her shoulder length dark hair had been pulled into a loose chignon at the nape of her neck and she wore her flower on the left side of her head. Mo turned to watch her twin flame walk slowly towards her, supported by her father who, like her own family, leant their blessing to this union.

At the reception and the formalities over Mo cornered Jake.

"I think that speech was Jaime's handiwork, far too complimentary for your acid sense of humour."

"There's a time and place for everything Mo, and this was neither the time nor place for my acerbic wit. So yes, I have to admit I can't claim it as all my own work," he bent to kiss her cheek. "Glad to officially welcome you into the Summers' family, sister-in-law."

She laughed. "Well thank you kindly Guv, and I suppose as a relation of the Connolly clan you expect premium discount when you get that classic car renovation you're always talking about."

He laughed out loud. "We're being watched."

She followed his eyes and saw the two Mason sisters smiling over at them. "I've mingled enough, time to get back to my bride, get changed and prepare for the evening session with friends, family and fun. Thanks, Jake, for helping to make this the best day of my life."

"You're very welcome DI Connolly and I promise they'll be no frantic calls to the Maldives demanding your immediate return to work."

63

They think I'm insane, not so. I merely host the seed of insanity bequeathed by an ancestor I knew nothing of and first brought to life by a father determined to nurture the legacy. I am now the embodiment and the evil that was once Jeb Carter. Paul Jamieson was innocent of any crime, just an unfortunate victim of circumstance. Deemed unfit to plead I'll be found guilty in my absence, of that I'm sure. Can they not see I had no choice but to do what I did. Born with the wrong DNA, made worse by an unnatural childhood and festering resentment for a lifestyle denied to me, married to a woman who despised me for not being her much adored father, surely they must see I had no choice.

I'll die in an asylum amongst the truly insane and they expect Jeb Carter's legacy to die with me. I have no heirs but they've forgotten Clive, Carter Jamieson's bastard son, conceived through violence and at 37 young enough to father innumerable sons and heirs. He's visited several times since learning of his true parentage, guilty I suppose of having the happy childhood denied to me. But there is a certain fascination too; his questions about our father assure me of that. He carries Jeb Carter's genetic footprint, albeit diluted by lifestyle, and could so easily perpetuate his accursed heritage. I cannot foretell the future but I'm convinced that Jeb will not die with me. His evil will linger on, waiting to infect some other wretched being.

Psychiatrists will come and go, diagnose one or another form of mental illness but thy will never see or believe in the evil spirit that lurks within.

So say not goodbye to Jeb but a cautionary farewell.

EPILOGUE

KATE

Increasingly disturbed by the thought that I was responsible for releasing the monster that was Jeb Carter into the 21st Century to create murder and mayhem, I sought the advice and solicitude of my teacher and mentor Francesca Whitely. Francesca is a world renowned Psychic Medium with a huge following, every venue at which she appears is packed to the rafters. Eighteen-months ago Linda dragged me to such a meeting in the Corn Exchange, Newbury. I was amazed that Francesca commanded such an on stage presence. She was a slight woman in her late fifties with long unruly grey hair, unremarkable to look at but she had the ability to capture and hold her audience's interest throughout the evening. It was made memorable for me when towards the end of the evening Francesca asked "is there a Kate in the audience?"

I put up my hand, as did two others in the auditorium.

"I have Tommy here, he's in uniform and walks with a distinctive limp. He's telling you to be happy. That your life will move on from the recent split with a loved one. That you'll begin to find your purpose in life as your spiritual journey begins."

I immediately recognised my beloved grandfather, who lost a leg in the D-Day landings in 1944. My hand stayed firmly in the air, the other two had long since disappeared.

Francesca smiled. "So Kate, you relate to our guest. Then come and see me after the meeting, we have things to discuss."

And that's how I met my mentor Francesca Whitely. My grandfather had asked her to guide me through my spiritual journey and to my utter astonishment she had agreed. Who better than the best in the business. A respected Medium, Francesca is also a trained clinical hypnotherapist so as well as being my spiritual sage she has trained me in Past Life Regression and other hypnotherapy techniques.

In one of the first conversations I ever had with her she said, "what I'm about to tell you stays between us."

I nodded my assent.

"There are charlatans in every business, none more so than ours. If you want to be a 'fairground fortune teller' (her name for those in the business that exploit people for financial gain) then I am not the teacher for you. The life I live is not one on an ego trip: I live with my two cats in a two-bedroomed cottage overlooking Chesil Beach, just outside the village of Burton Bradstock on the Dorset coast. Half the money I make I give to worthy causes in the places I visit. From the other half I pay expenses and the remainder is enough for my modest needs. I want to help people not exploit them."

"I'm with you 100%," I said, happy to learn from such an honourable woman.

We meet twice yearly at her cottage in Dorset, take long walks on the beach, meditate together and engage in meaningful conversation about my spiritual development. Every couple of months we talk on Skype, more if I need to consult her.

I digress, but I feel the background to our relationship needs to be understood. The trust between us is paramount and I know although it can only be her view, she will guide me to the best of her experience. So I told her about my involvement in the case and about the feelings of guilt and self- doubt that were plaguing me before asking the question that was so important to me.

"Can spirit be reincarnated in the same family, generations apart?"

She thought for a minute before answering.

"Honestly, I doubt it. We all belong to soul groups and are often re-incarnated with other members of that group, but I have never experienced a situation where spirit has been reincarnated into a genetic descendant. My opinion, for what it's worth, is that Jamieson was not a reincarnation of Jeb Carter. Carter was merely an ancestor forced into his twisted mind by constant exposure and a lot of research. However, I don't know everything and maybe it is possible, but even if it were you are in no way to blame. You followed procedure by telling him to close the door to his past behind him, if he ignored you it's his problem not yours. Be assured, he has a troubled mind and that was not as a result of the past life regression, more a genetic time bomb waiting to explode."

As always I'm grateful for having this wise and knowledgeable woman as my friend and mentor.

ABOUT THE AUTHOR

Trish Harland was born 70-years ago in the small market town of Huntingdon. Her career as a research scientist brought her to Oxfordshire in 1992 when she relocated to Wantage, where she still lives with her family and two cats. Writing has always been an interest and you can find poems and short stories littered around her home. She has always wanted to write a novel and started her first book, albeit half-heartedly, when she retired in 2005.

Printed in Great Britain
by Amazon.co.uk, Ltd.,
Marston Gate.